The Beach Dogs

By the same author

The Beach Dogs

COLIN DANN

Hutchinson
London Melbourne Auckland Johannesburg

Copyright © Colin Dann 1988

All rights reserved

First published in Great Britain in 1988
by Hutchinson Children's Books
An imprint of Century Hutchinson Ltd
Brookmount House, 62–65 Chandos Place,
Covent Garden, London WC2N 4NW

Century Hutchinson Australia (Pty) Ltd
16–22 Church Street, Hawthorn, Melbourne, Victoria 3122

Century Hutchinson New Zealand Limited
32–34 View Road, PO Box 40–086, Glenfield, Auckland 10

Century Hutchinson South Africa (Pty) Ltd
PO Box 337, Bergvlei 2012, South Africa

Set in Baskerville by BookEns, Saffron Walden, Essex

Printed and bound in Great Britain by
Anchor Brendon Ltd, Tiptree, Essex

British Library Cataloguing in Publication Data

Dann, Colin
The beach dogs.
I. Title
823'.914[J]

ISBN 0-09-173623-4

Contents

For Anna and Sarah

1

The Café Dog

The seaside resort of Multon is not very big. It has a short pier with an amusement arcade and a kiosk at the end selling souvenirs, ice cream, rock and candy floss. There are also a putting green, a crazy golf course, tennis courts, a paddling pool for toddlers, some guest houses, a few shops, two pubs and a café. The main reason people go to Multon is not so much for these modest attractions but because of the town's situation. It lies at one end of a broad bay, sheltered from the wind, and the sea around it is comfortably warm throughout the summer. Bathing there is a delight and, at the height of the season, Multon is thronged with visitors. There are boat trips across the bay and also to the island of Clany, about half an hour distant. Only a small number of people live on this island and most of them are monks, hidden away in the monastery which has been established on Clany for centuries.

The esplanade at Multon follows the curve of the bay and is lined by fishermen's cottages, most of which are now converted into shops or guest houses. Near the entrance to the pier, some years ago, one of the cottages was turned into the Seagull Café. This was owned for thirty years by the same proprietors, Mr and Mrs Clements. Every morning during the season the café door was opened by Mr Clements at exactly half-past eight. Not to let in the first customers of the day, because there were never any around so early, but to let out a little white rough-haired terrier called Zoe. Zoe was a West Highland White, a Christmas present one year from Mr and Mrs Clements' son to his parents. She was rather an unlooked-for Christmas present since the owners of the Seagull Café were not too happy about keeping a dog in a place where food was served all day. So they decided that during the hours when the café was open, Zoe would have to be put outside. And when it was closed, or if the weather turned very cold, she would only be allowed into their living quarters above the café.

Zoe got quite used to this and usually made a beeline for the steps leading down from the promenade to the beach, especially in wet weather when she would shelter under the pier. She liked to roam around the shingle, exploring the new scents her inquisitive nose picked up each day. She made friends with another dog, Bertram, who was often to be found on the beach too. But whereas Zoe was still young and full of energy, Bertram was old and spent a lot of time sleeping. Then she would leave him and wander off on her own. It was because of this, more than anything else, that one September, late in the season, they embarked on an adventure which was to have consequences neither of them expected.

2

The Pier End Dog

Bertram was a boxer. His brindled coat was grizzled; he was overweight and wheezy; in fact if he exerted himself too much his breathing became quite laboured. He belonged to Mr Locke, the owner of the pier kiosk. As Bertram grew older, Mr Locke's wife used to remark that the dog smelt, and so her husband had to take him to the kiosk every day in the season to get him away from the house. There was no room for a big dog inside the hut, so most days Bertram waddled along the pier to the steps down to the beach and made his way to a favourite spot. This was a patch of sand amongst the pebbles that caught the sun for most of the day and so remained warm and cosy. Zoe was always on the beach before Bertram. Sometimes he couldn't find her straight away and he would bark once or twice to call her. Then he'd soon see her, trotting briskly towards him in her perky way, her bright black eyes gleaming like buttons and her white coat always looking as if it had just been brushed. Bertram was very fond of Zoe, in a fatherly, indulgent sort of way. He was fourteen years old, and felt it was his duty to look after the little terrier. He knew that Zoe liked him very much too but was only too aware that he wasn't lively enough for her, and this realization always gave him a pang.

One particular morning in late September Bertram

and Zoe met as usual. It was a bright crisp day and Zoe stood by a breakwater snuffling the air and savouring all the delicious scents carried on the breeze. 'There's no warmth in the day,' Bertram grumbled. The chill in the air told him the season was coming to its end and he felt morose. He knew that he and Zoe wouldn't be able to see each other for much longer. For although the Seagull Café stayed open throughout the year, Mr Locke closed the kiosk in the winter months as Multon's tourists vanished until the spring.

Zoe didn't reply. She wasn't interested in weather changes, when there were much more absorbing things to investigate. Then she said, 'I've been speaking to the other dog again.'

'Oh, have you?' said Bertram. He was a little envious of 'the other dog', a black and white terrier-shaped mongrel who was full of stories and seemed to have lots of fun with Zoe. 'You don't want to believe everything he tells you.'

'He was telling me about his master's house on the island,' Zoe answered, 'so he had no need to make that up.'

The mongrel spent most of his time riding around in a boat belonging to his master, a retired seaman who now made a living ferrying passengers around the bay or across to Clany and back.

Bertram yawned and tried to change the subject. He thought the mongrel was too rough and ready to be a fit companion for Zoe. 'Let's walk under the pier and up to the rocks,' he suggested. Zoe knew this would take them away from the part of the beach where the boat lay waiting for the day's first customers. She wouldn't be diverted.

'I don't know why you're not more friendly to that dog,' she said. 'He can be a lot of fun. All *we* do is talk about our owners.'

'Not all the time,' Bertram protested. But he had to admit they often compared notes about their owners' lack of interest in them.

'We haven't much longer together this year,' Bertram wheedled. 'Can't it just be the two of us till I go?'

'Oh come on, then,' Zoe relented. 'Let's run.'

Bertram bit back the answer, 'You know I can't' and struggled gamely after her little white figure as she scampered over the pebbles. It wasn't long however, before he had to pause for breath, his old sides heaving, watching her diminish into a tiny speck in the distance. Zoe soon noticed she wasn't followed and came dancing back, for she wasn't unkind. 'I'm sorry,' she said. 'I forgot again.'

Bertram was still gasping for breath. 'I used to . . . run like the . . . wind,' he panted. 'You wouldn't think . . . so now.'

'I wish I'd known you then,' said Zoe wistfully, 'Jack can run and leap in a flash – you should see him chase a ball.'

'Who's Jack anyway?' Bertram asked grudgingly, knowing the answer already.

'The other dog, the one that—'

'Yes, yes, I know,' Bertram interrupted, 'Jack. Sounds like the right sort of name for a rough and tumble character like him.'

'Come on, you've got your breath back,' said Zoe impatiently, and led him down to the water's edge. The sea glittered in the early morning sunlight, as Zoe chased the ripples that ran inshore. Bertram sighed. She was so full of vigour while he—

'How d'you know we haven't got much longer together?' she asked him suddenly, interrupting his thoughts.

'As I said, it's less warm,' he reminded her. 'The darkness comes sooner, and surely you've noticed that there are far fewer humans around now? All this tells me my master will soon be leaving the pier and not coming back for a long time.'

'Aren't you clever?' Zoe flattered him, though she really did think so. Bertram loved her to praise him. His spirits lifted as he stumped through the wavelets. 'When you've been around as long as I have, Zoe,' he muttered, 'you'll—'

'Oh, *no one's* been around as long as you have,' she teased, but she said it so prettily that Bertram wasn't hurt, only amused. Then he remembered the kennels.

'I hate it when my master leaves the pier,' he told Zoe. 'He and my mistress always go away and abandon me for an age, shacked up with a lot of strangers in kennels. There's no peace or privacy; noise from morning till night and herded together for walks like a lot of sheep.'

'I've never been in kennels,' said Zoe.

'I hope you never will be.'

They went on to the rocks and sniffed at the deep pools left by the tide. Zoe surprised a shore crab and ran after it as it scuttled away along the sand. She came back to tell Bertram, 'Jack lives on the island all the time when his master stops working.'

Bertram didn't care what he did. 'Jack this, Jack that,' he mimicked. 'There was a time when you were quite content with my company. We didn't need anyone else.'

Zoe stared at him. 'You're an old grumbler,' she said. 'I think I'll go off if you don't cheer up.'

'Do what you like, Zoe,' he muttered. 'I'm going to have a lie down.'

'Oh, not already!' she exclaimed, but Bertram paid no attention and settled himself well away from any uncomfortable pebbles. His old body needed its comfort. Zoe watched him with irritation, feeling Bertram was deliberately trying to annoy her. Soon he'd be dozing again. She turned away and set off determinedly back in the direction of the pier.

3

The Boat-trip Dog

Jack, the black-and-white mongrel, was lying by his master's hut. He had been fed and now his owner, known to everyone as Seaman Halebury, was having his breakfast. Jack blinked lazily in the sun, enjoying a rare moment of stillness. There would soon be plenty to do. When the first queue of customers formed for a boat trip, Jack knew his work was about to begin. He would run up and down the shingle alongside the catwalk the passengers used to keep their feet dry as they filed into the small craft. He believed he was shepherding them inside and, once they were all in, he would jump on to the raised plank himself and trot nonchalantly along it to take his place in the small cabin for the length of the voyage. He always went to the same corner, like clockwork, and he had the air of being far more familiar with boats and sailing than any of the passengers. The *Crest* was a small craft with a noisy, sputtering engine. It tended to roll and pitch in even a moderate swell, but Jack understood its every movement and he felt very much as though it was *his* boat.

Now the Crest rocked gently at its moorings and Jack's wiry, elastic body, about the size of a fox terrier, was for the moment quiet. He watched Zoe approaching. He liked her a lot, above all because he loved an audience. As she came near he sprang to his feet, wagging his tail.

'Back again, eh?' he cried. 'Where's the old feller, your companion?'

'Bertram's by the rock pools. Sleeping, I expect.'

'Oh well, that's age for you,' Jack said. 'Can't blame him, eh?'

'He can be a bit of a moaner at times,' Zoe confided. 'Although,' she added loyally, 'I've a great affection for him.'

''Course you have,' Jack agreed. 'Bound to. Known him a long while, haven't you.'

'Yes.'

'What's he moaning about? The master?'

'Sort of. He feels our beach days are almost over for this year and he's dreading being cooped up.'

'Cooped up? What – indoors, you mean?'

'His owners put him in kennels, whatever they are. He hates it.'

'I've heard of them,' said Jack. 'Poor old Bertram. But it has got quiet, hasn't it? I think he's right about the end for this year. When my master packs up we'll be going to the island for a spell. What happens to you?'

'Oh, I get shut up most of the time myself,' said Zoe. 'But my owners'll keep working. I'll be forgotten about upstairs.'

'Sounds dull,' said Jack. 'Listen, I've got an idea. Fancy a boat trip some time?'

Zoe's eyes shone with excitement. 'Oh!' she cried. 'When? How? Where?'

'Hold on, hold on,' Jack answered with amusement. 'Let me think about it. You could bring the old'un too.'

'Oh, *he* wouldn't come.'

'How d'you know? Have you asked him?'

'But where would we go? Tell me!' Zoe begged.

'Ever been to the island?'

'No, never.'

'Like to go? Lots to explore there if you don't know it. There's a giant—'

'A giant!'

'Yes – huge.' Jack could see he was impressing her and began to elaborate. 'Bertram's a big dog but he'd look like a pup by the side of it. Ever seen a giant?'

'No. I don't know what you mean.'

'You will when you see it.' Jack's ears pricked up. He'd heard a sound. 'Ah, my master's stirring. He'll be calling me. You go and tell Bertram my idea and I'll think how we can do it. Meet me tomorrow!'

Seaman Halebury stepped out of his hut and stretched. He gave a greeting to Zoe whom he recognized, but she ran off as she was a bit afraid of him.

Bertram was still lying by the rocks. He wasn't asleep and he was pleased when Zoe reappeared. 'Finished your nap?' she enquired sarcastically. 'I've got news.'

'I don't spend as much time sleeping as you try to make out,' the old boxer defended himself. 'What news?'

'We're to go on a voyage.'

Bertram gaped.

'We're invited on a boat trip, my dear old friend,' said Zoe enthusiastically. 'Jack wants to show us the island. There's a giant there!'

Bertram ignored her last announcement, looking disdainful. 'What a silly idea,' he declared. 'As if we'd want to do such a thing!'

'But I do want to!' Zoe cried crossly. 'Of course I do. It's more exciting than lolling about here all day moaning,' she added pointedly.

'Oh, I see. You want to. Well, why tell me then?'

Zoe was piqued. She actually wanted Bertram's company on the boat because she wasn't sure how Jack's owner would react to some extra passengers. 'Oh, you always spoil things,' she accused him. '*You're* invited too. Jack said to meet him tomorrow to talk about how we should go about it. Oh, Bertram, do come with me. I don't think I'd go by myself.'

Bertram felt better when Zoe showed she needed him. 'I'm not committing myself,' he said, 'but I'll come and see this Jack with you to find out what he's up to.'

'He's not up to anything,' Zoe answered. 'He thought we'd enjoy the change. There's so much to explore there and – and – the giant! Have you seen a giant before?'

'Hm! Giant!' Bertram scoffed. 'You don't want to believe everything he tells you, Zoe. He loves to spin you a yarn, I know.'

At midday Mr Locke from the pier kiosk and Mr Clements from the Seagull Café emerged to call their dogs back. Zoe was given some biscuits and water or milk at this time; her main meal was in the evening. Bertram had one large meal a day and that was at lunch-time. Mrs Locke preferred him to be fed away from the house, as she said he made such a mess of his food, so Mr Locke kept a supply of dog food at the back of his kiosk and added to it any scraps or leftovers of meat from the house, and there was always a bowl of water for Bertram outside it. The two owners often bumped into each other on the beach. They knew each other well, not only because of their pets, but also because they had worked close by for so many years. Naturally they were familiar with Seaman Halebury too, but Mr Clements didn't have much to do with him and so didn't appreciate just what Jack's company would mean for Zoe. If he had, he might not have allowed her to run around quite so freely.

4

When the Season Ends....

That afternoon was warm and even Zoe felt drowsy. She lay with her head on her paws, her small body pressed against Bertram's bulk in his favourite sunny spot. Jack and the *Crest* had come and gone many times before the time came for the two friends to be taken home for the evening. 'I'll see you under the pier, early,' was the boxer's parting remark as Mr Locke stood jangling Bertram's lead at the top of the steps.

Zoe was first at the appointed place the next morning, eager to reach Jack and hear his plan. She couldn't keep still for excitement about the proposed trip and ran up and down as she waited for Bertram, trying to think of how she could persuade the old dog to accompany her. When at last Bertram came plodding and snorting down the steps, Zoe rushed up to him. 'About time,' she said impatiently. 'Any longer and Jack will be gone. I thought you said "early".'

'Don't make a fuss,' mumbled the old dog. 'I can't get here before my master lets me.'

Zoe was already on her way, trotting along. 'Come *on*, Bertram,' she called over her shoulder.

Jack had been keeping a look-out and came halfway to meet them. 'Just in time – I haven't got long. The master's getting my food,' he said hurriedly. 'Are you both coming, then?'

'Coming where?' Bertram asked, making himself sound as uninterested as possible.

'The trip, the trip,' Zoe reminded him irritably.

'To the island, you know,' Jack added. 'I don't think you've been there?'

'No, I haven't been there; can't think why I'd want to,' Bertram answered. 'I've no desire to go on any voyage at my time of life.' He looked away with a supercilious expression as if the younger dog's plans were quite beneath him.

'Suit yourself,' Jack said. 'But you're missing a wonderful chance to explore and—'

'Explore?' Bertram interrupted. 'I'm too old to explore.'

'Oh, Bertram, you're so unadventurous!' Zoe exclaimed with exasperation. 'You're not *so* decrepit. Won't you come for my sake?'

Bertram didn't respond, but Zoe's appeal had its effect. If she really wanted him along. . . . But no, he mustn't give in too easily and lose his dignity.

'Don't worry about him, Zoe,' Jack said brightly. 'Let him do as he likes. We'll still have fun, just the two of us.'

Bertram began to realize his staying behind would not be such a good thing. He didn't want Zoe to become so friendly with lively young Jack that she no longer had any time for him. He looked back at the little white dog, and her beseeching expression did the trick.

'Oh, very well,' said Bertram. 'Count me in. I'd be bored to death here on my own anyway.'

'Lovely, lovely,' cried Zoe, skipping about, her stub of a tail wagging with delight.

'One thing though, er, Jack,' Bertram continued. 'What about your master? *He* wouldn't allow us on your boat, I'm sure.'

Zoe was glad to hear this question: Jack's master was the one snag in the whole scheme.

'Don't see why not,' Jack answered abruptly. 'As long as we all keep out of the way.'

'No, no,' Bertram argued. 'I don't believe he would. I know humans, they don't like strange dogs in their territory. *My* mistress doesn't even like her own dog in hers. If Zoe and I are to come we shall have to be hidden somewhere.' He was quite insistent. Zoe thought again how wise he was and how no harm could befall her in this adventure as long as he was around.

'We-ell,' Jack mused, 'perhaps you're right. I'll have to think about that. It'd be difficult for you to get into the boat without being seen.' He gave a sudden leap, turning his supple body in mid-air and landing neatly. Zoe was impressed, as he had meant her to be.

'Let's have a run round,' Jack said briskly. 'It'll help me to think.' He raced off in the direction of the tide, bounding and vaulting over the pebbles as if he were made of rubber. He turned once to make sure Zoe was following. Bertram didn't attempt to compete but sat down where he was and watched the young dogs' vigour with envy. They ran, circling each other, jumping and spinning with exhilaration. Bertram felt very left out. He could still recall what it had been like to be so full of energy he couldn't be still for more than a moment. So long ago, so long ago. . . . It was horrible being old and breathless and stiff-legged and – unwanted? The thought crept into the boxer's mind almost of itself. No. He shook it away with an actual toss of his head; mustn't think like that. And yet, his mistress . . . she didn't love him. And the kennels. Oh, how he loathed them. It wasn't fair to put an old dog like him to such discomfort.

Jack and Zoe disturbed his thoughts as they came

bouncing back. 'You look very glum, old feller,' Jack remarked. 'What's up?'

'Oh – nothing,' Bertram answered miserably.

'Of course there's something,' said Zoe. 'Out with it, Bertram.' Her black button eyes gleamed.

'Just the future, I suppose.'

'Oh, I see. The kennels, you mean?'

'Yes.'

Jack made one of his sudden springs into the air. 'Hey – listen!' he cried. 'What an idea I've had! Why don't you stay on the island like me? Then there'd be no kennels!'

'What – what do you mean?' Bertram mumbled.

'When my master's work is done here we go to the island,' Jack explained. 'We live there all the time when the season's over. Well – why don't *you*? There are Good People on the island. They look after all sorts of animals. You and Zoe would be welcome and – and – we could all go around together. My master lets me run free most of the time. I'll show you the giant and where to sleep and where you must go to be fed and – everything!'

'I'd do anything to avoid the kennels,' Bertram admitted. 'But Zoe, what do you think?'

'Better than being shut up,' she said at once. 'I'll be locked away too, once cold weather comes.'

'What *of* the cold?' Bertram was suddenly reminded. 'I can't stand it, you see, at my age. Last winter my mistress relented and let me indoors when it was really bad. How would we manage on the island?'

'Oh, there's plenty of shelter,' Jack answered dismissively. 'No problem there. Now then, I think I've solved everything. When my master's finished ferrying people about the boat is empty and there's plenty of room to hide. I know just the place.'

Zoe and Bertram exchanged glances. They felt as if they were now caught up in something neither of them could stop.

'How will you know when all the boat trips are over?' Bertram asked shrewdly. 'Your master makes so many of them.'

'Ah!' Jack exclaimed as if realizing for the first time that the boxer was no fool. He looked at Bertram's grizzled, furrowed face. One of the older dog's eyes was watering and a long tear ran down through the wrinkles and mingled with the general wetness of his blunt nose. 'There *is* a way I can tell,' Jack said conspiratorially. 'My master collects together all the things from his hut on the mainland and loads them into his boat. I always know when he does that it means our work's over and we're to have a long rest.'

'You mustn't forget to tell us,' said Zoe. 'It could be any time now.'

'Don't worry, I won't,' Jack assured her. 'It may be quite soon. But you won't miss the boat!' He leapt up and tried to somersault in the air.

'Jack! Jack!' Seaman Halebury was calling. The mongrel ran off without another word. He was hungry.

'He's not so bad,' Bertram remarked as he watched Jack vanish. 'Perhaps I didn't do him justice. But I wish he wouldn't caper about so much.'

Zoe wasn't listening. Her mind was full of the island, the giant and the Good People.

5

To the Island

Over the following days Zoe watched the dwindling. number of visitors around Multon carefully. She wondered if they would all have to disappear before Jack's master would decide to leave. But, after a little over a week, the mongrel sought out Zoe and Bertram urgently one late afternoon. He came scampering over the pebbles to them as they lay dozing in the boxer's favourite spot.

'Can't stop,' he panted. 'Be ready. My master's clearing out. Come to the boat at dark. I'll find a way of distracting him – make him take me for a walk.'

Zoe jumped up. 'Where do we hide?'

'The rear of the boat,' Jack told her. 'Taupaulins – you know, covers. My master drapes them over his clutter. You must find a space – burrow under them.' He bounded off without further ado before either of the dogs could ask him anything more.

Bertram clambered to his feet. 'We can't stay on the beach until dark,' he protested to Zoe, swaying slightly on his bandy legs. 'We'll be collected long before.'

'Oh no, we won't,' declared the West Highland White.

'What – what do you mean?'

'We won't *be* here to be collected,' Zoe yapped impatiently. 'Will we?'

'No. No – well, of course we mustn't be,' Bertram stammered. 'Now then' – he tried to take charge – 'we must – er – go somewhere else.'

'Oh Bertram!' cried Zoe. 'Is that all you can say? Have you no ideas?'

'The rock pools? No. That's not far enough,' the boxer answered himself in the same breath. He'd begun to wheeze. 'They'd find us there. Have to be farther than that. Let's see now – I know!' he barked triumphantly.

'What? What?'

'Follow me, Zoe,' Bertram directed and, with an unaccustomed bustle in his movements, lumbered over the shingle to the pier and steps. Zoe trotted in his wake obediently. She had never seen him so active. Once on the promenade he looked quickly round. No sign of his owner, nor of Mr Clements. Stiff-legged, he hurried off in the direction of the crazy golf course and the Cliff Gardens, turning just once to make sure that Zoe was still behind him.

The dogs aroused little interest among the handful of people who were about, most of whom were bent on hurrying home for their tea. Bertram led the way into the Gardens and made for a particularly thick group of flowering shrubs. Amongst these they were well screened.

'How did you know about this place?' Zoe asked.

'Oh, I'm sometimes exercised up here,' Bertram answered.

'Are you? I've never been here,' Zoe confessed. 'My master never takes me on a good walk.' Not for the first time she felt aggrieved. Her mistress would spend hours washing and combing Zoe's coat, which the little dog loathed, yet she never considered giving her an outing – something that would really have pleased her. She was not well looked after.

'As soon as it's really dark, we must slip out,' Bertram

told her. 'And we'll have to take great care because our owners will be searching for us.'

'I hadn't thought of that,' said Zoe, with just a hint of regret.

'You're not having second thoughts?'

'No.' Zoe pictured Jack waiting vainly by the boat. What would he think of her? She fondly imagined his distress. But supposing, just supposing her owners might also be distressed? No; it seemed impossible and she shook the thought away. No, she wouldn't be missed.

Dusk fell slowly, maddeningly slowly. Or perhaps it just appeared to the two dogs that way because they were waiting for it. They lingered in the gloom until their patience ran out.

'Surely it's dark enough now?' Zoe begged fretfully.

'Yes,' said Bertram. 'Yes, I think so. Keep with me.' He stepped from the foliage and sniffed cautiously. Zoe aped him, wrinkling her little black nose.

'All clear,' Bertram grunted and set off back to the esplanade. He avoided the pier and made a wide detour which brought them to a point much farther along the sea front, beyond Seaman Halebury's shed and his beloved *Crest*. All the time he scanned the neighbourhood for signs of his and Zoe's owners. Bertram's eyes were not as sharp as they had been, but his nose more than made up for this. No scent escaped it.

'So far so good,' he whispered to Zoe whose white coat was rather too conspicuous among the shadows. They peered through the promenade railings at the beach. There were no steps here for them to run down. 'We'll have to jump,' said Bertram.

'Is – is it far?' Zoe asked nervously.

'Not too bad,' he answered, 'and if my old legs can do it, yours should easily manage the drop. Quickly now!' He scrambled under the lower bar of the railings, teetered a moment on the edge of the embankment and, with a stiff sort of kick of his back legs, launched himself forward. He landed in a heap on the thickly piled pebbles, none the worse for his leap. Zoe heard the crash and bounded after him. Without a word Bertram led her off across the shingle, towards the *Crest*.

Ever since dusk, Jack had been keeping a watch for his friends. His master had almost finished piling his paraphernalia in the boat, but there was no time now for a walk. In fact there would only be one opportunity for Bertram and Zoe to get aboard undetected. That would be when Seaman Halebury had finished stowing his gear and was in the wheelhouse, preparing to start the boat's engine. Timing would be everything. Jack followed his master's movements as he trudged to and from the shed, paddling in his sea-boots to the stern of the *Crest* with load after load of clutter. He was afraid Bertram and Zoe might be picked up before they could get to him. But at last he saw the terrier's white blur approaching through the warm, early-October night. Bertram's bulk loomed into view immediately afterwards.

Jack skipped forward.

'Lie low!' he hissed. 'There – behind the shed!'

They followed his directions, pressing themselves doggo against the shingle. Zoe's heart thumped expectantly. They heard Halebury's footsteps approaching, some bumps inside the shed, then footsteps going away again. They had arrived in the nick of time, for the man returned only once more, to bang the shed door shut and lock it.

'Come on, Jack!' they heard him call, not waiting to see if the mongrel followed. They hesitated, but then Jack ran up.

'Now!' he snapped urgently. 'Down to the water's edge! You'll see the covers in the rear of the boat. As soon

as you hear the engine start, jump in and get out of sight!'
He dashed off again before his master came back to see
where he'd gone.

Bertram and Zoe trod warily through the darkness
towards the hulk of the boat, bobbing low in the water.
The catwalk had been removed, and they saw Jack leap
nimbly on board.

'I can't do that!' Bertram exclaimed in alarm. 'What
does he think I am – a puppy?!'

'You can't give up now, Bertram,' Zoe protested. 'It's
too late!' Even as she answered, the engine kicked into
life, and she raced the last few metres and hurled herself
over the stern. Bertram lumbered up in a panic. Zoe was
already out of sight but Jack had seen her and now he
stood, waiting for the boxer to board, and silently
encouraging him. The shadowy figure of Halebury was
visible at the wheel.

'Quickly!' Jack hissed. 'There's not a moment to
spare.'

In desperation Bertram made a lunge for the side and
managed to get his front legs over. His hind legs kicked
feebly in the air; he was half in and half out of the boat.
Suddenly the engine roared and the *Crest* lurched and
swung away, pitching Bertram unceremoniously on to
the deck. Shaken but triumphant he crawled to the tarpaulin and pushed himself underneath. Drowned by the
noise of the engine, the dogs' movements went unheard
by the captain of the *Crest*, who knew nothing of his
strange stowaways.

Bertram and Zoe found each other under the covering.
Zoe was relieved that the old boxer had made it and she
could now give full sway to her feelings of excitement.
The throbbing of the engine was like the pulse of adventure coursing through her body. Restless and quivering,
she longed to run wild in the open.

'When do we get to the island?' she asked impatiently.

'How should I know?' Bertram retorted, but he had caught some of Zoe's enthusiasm too.

A little later Jack came nosing warily beneath the tarpaulin. 'Listen, I can't stay long,' he began. 'You'll have to move before we land on the other side. As soon as you hear the engine stop, you must come out – but carefully – and jump into the water. We row to shore in a dinghy, but you'll have to swim the last little bit to shore if you don't want to be seen.'

'Swim!' exclaimed Bertram. 'You never warned us of this. Supposing we—'

Jack interrupted him. 'Don't suppose anything, old feller. The sea's as calm as a pond; you'll have no trouble at all. It'll just be a little paddle.'

'Where should we go then?' Zoe asked breathlessly.

'There's plenty of hiding-places near the shore,' Jack told her. 'There are caves – you know, hidey-holes – but it might be better to go to the scrub by the shore and stay there until daylight. I'll meet you there tomorrow; you'll be perfectly safe till I come. Then I can explain to you about the Good People and how they'll feed you. Good luck!' He scurried away.

'It's all right for him, isn't it?' Bertram muttered. 'Bet he won't even get his feet wet.'

'Do – do you think we'll see the – giant?' Zoe panted. In her mind she was already on the island.

'Giant be blowed!' Bertram replied with feeling. 'I'm more interested in where our next meal comes from. My stomach's beginning to nag.'

'We won't get anything until tomorrow,' Zoe reminded him. 'You'll have to ignore it.'

They lapsed into silence. On the *Crest*'s clock the minutes ticked past: ten, twenty, thirty. . . . Then, abruptly, the engine cut out and the *Crest* slid silently over the water as she approached the landing-stage at Clany harbour. Bertram and Zoe heaved themselves into the open. Seaman Halebury was busy manoeuvring his craft on the tide, the stern of the boat bathed in moonlight. The dogs took advantage of her rocking motion and dropped over the side as the boat dipped toward the sea. Zoe's little body made almost no sound as it hit the water. Bertram's heavier bulk splashed loudly, but the unexpected noise went unnoticed. Jack heard it and was happy; he looked forward to showing off his home territory to his two visitors.

Bertram and Zoe were surprised by the warmth of the water, for the sea had had all summer to warm up. They dog paddled their way to the dark shore. It was as easy as Jack had forecast and, in five minutes, they were on land and shaking themselves vigorously. They had almost enjoyed their swim.

Bertram cast about for shelter. Behind the flat sandy foreshore was a rocky promontory which slid down at a sharp angle towards the beach. An easy path led up to some thick vegetation, where gorse, bracken, broom and brambles offered a perfect resting-place. The two dogs were soon well hidden. They were high enough up to overlook the jetty and were able to watch Jack and his master disembark and walk to a footpath that led up the hillside in another direction. There were one or two fishermen about but, apart from them, all was quiet.

'Jack's going home,' said Zoe.

'Yes – home to be fed, I bet,' Bertram said ruefully. He felt uncomfortable. Never before in his fourteen years had he ever missed a meal. He tried not to think of his big food-bowl at home which was filled to the brim each lunchtime, even if some of the scraps it contained didn't always take his fancy.

The *Crest* bobbed at her mooring, still weighed down

by the miscellaneous junk from Halebury's shed, for it was too dark for the seaman to unload now. In Multon, the pier kiosk had closed for another year: Bertram had escaped the kennels by the skin of his teeth. His and Zoe's owners were at that moment searching vainly for their missing pets.

Zoe pushed herself against the damp warmth of Bertram's body. She hadn't slept in the open before at night and the old boxer's hide gave her comfort. The excitement and the energetic start to their adventure had tired her out, and she was soon asleep; even when Bertram began to snore she didn't wake up.

6

A Giant

The sun was shining brightly when Zoe woke again. For a moment she couldn't understand what had happened. What on earth was she doing next to Bertram in her sleeping-basket? Then she heard the sound of the sea, smelt the sharp tang of seaweed and a dozen other fresh scents and jumped up. A branch of gorse prickled her back, even through her thick hair. She gave a little yelp and saw Bertram open his eyes. He yawned, stretched where he lay, still on his side, then slowly turned his head and saw Zoe. He showed no surprise, for he could think of nothing except an overwhelming feeling of hunger. Happily the dogs soon discovered that Jack hadn't deserted them. They had scarcely got used to their new surroundings before the mongrel appeared, jumping through the ferns. He barked to them joyfully, his curled tail wagging frantically.

'Hallo! Here I am! Oh, it's wonderful to see you both here.'

Zoe shook herself fully awake and barked a greeting. 'Clever Jack,' she said. 'How easily you found us.'

'I picked up your scents quite soon,' he said. 'Well, Bertram,' he said to the boxer, 'didn't everything go perfectly?'

'Pretty well,' Bertram allowed. 'Now what about—'

Jack was ahead of him. 'Say no more – I know your

thoughts,' he cried. 'Food! And quickly! Follow me.'

Full of vigour as usual he led them up the headland
behind their hiding-place. The scrub gave way to close-
cropped turf so springy underfoot that Jack and Zoe
danced over it in their delight. It was a wonderful day,
and even Bertram was in good fettle. The prospect of
being fed raised his spirits enormously as he ambled
along on his bow legs, doing his best to keep up with the
younger animals. A few sheep turned their heads at the
dogs' approach, but they apparently found them of no
interest and bent their heads down to the grass again.

'There are few animals here, and fewer people,' Jack
told Zoe. 'You'll be able to come and go as you like. No
one knows you except me and my master and we'll make
quite sure *he* doesn't see you.'

'What about the Good People? Are they expecting us?'
Zoe enquired innocently.

'No, no, they're not expecting you – well, not any more
than any other creature,' Jack replied. 'Hold still a
moment. Let's wait for Bertram and then I'll explain.'

The boxer trundled up, out of breath, but quite
unconcerned about it. 'Any animal – or bird – can come
to the Good People for food,' Jack went on. 'Each day
they put out food and water for those that need it. There
are other creatures who will be there; a few cats and
squirrels, but no stray dogs. The thing you must remember
is to go to the same place at the same time every day, so
that the Good People can see you. The food is provided
in the morning, early, always at the same time,' he
repeated. 'The cats never eat all the food and when they
see you they'll hold back anyway, if I know them, so
you'll get the best share. Now, let's go on, because it's
about time for feeding now.'

Zoe had a momentary qualm. 'The – the – giant
won't—' she began.

Jack was amused. 'Oh no, *he* never goes there; don't be alarmed. He finds his own food.'

Zoe looked puzzled. 'How does he do that?' she questioned. She only knew about food being provided for her and had never considered how birds, for instance, managed to feed themselves.

'It's a mystery,' Jack informed her. 'I've never seen the giant eat. But eat he does.'

Zoe was enthralled. 'Tell us more,' she urged Jack.

'Plenty of time for that later,' Bertrum grumbled. 'When *we've* eaten. "Never seen him eat",' he repeated scornfully. 'What a lot of nonsense!'

Jack didn't argue; Bertram would find out all in good time. By now, he had brought them to the inhabited part of the island: a few houses, a doctor's and a vet's surgery, a shop and post office and a café for visitors to the island. But the monastery, its chapel and outbuildings, dominated the little community. Jack padded along the narrow road confidently.

'Is your home around here?' Zoe asked.

'No. It's in quite another part of the island,' Jack answered. 'My master and I are rather isolated – we like it that way.'

They entered an archway in the wall surrounding the monastery and found themselves in a sort of enclosed courtyard. Three skinny cats were loitering in a patch of sun against one wall, but there were no other creatures visible.

'That's your competition,' Jack said, referring to the cats who were cowering uncertainly at the dogs' appearance.

'There *is* no competition,' said Bertram, contemptuously.

'But won't there be enough food for all?' Zoe asked. She had a kindly disposition and had no wish to oust the weaker animals from their habitual feeding place.

'I should think so,' Jack said, in a careless way. 'Depends on your appetites.'

'You can depend on mine,' Bertram remarked, jokingly.

Just then the clock at the top of the chapel belfry chimed nine times. At the sound the cats, all of whom were black, began to stir. They looked around expectantly, licking their chops, but didn't venture from their corner, although they could see that none of the dogs offered any threat.

A door opened in a far wall and a tall figure in a long, cream tasselled robe emerged, carrying dishes. The dogs' noses wrinkled appreciatively at the smell of food. In Jack's case the reaction was purely instinctive since he had already eaten, but Zoe and Bertram found it difficult not to rush forward. The man in the robe set the dishes down. He looked at the animals and decided to space the dishes out, clearly having doubts about how the cats and dogs would get on together. He went back through the door and presently returned with two empty bowls, which he filled with fresh water from a tap in another corner of the courtyard. Setting them down, he removed two bowls which were already under the tap, and then disappeared, taking the dirty bowls with him.

Zoe and Bertram hesitated; the cats did not. They made a beeline for the nearest dishes and began to eat in a hurried way.

'What are you waiting for?' Jack asked his companions. 'It may not be the sort of food you're used to being given but it's good enough – I've seen it. The Good People want to help you.'

Bertram lumbered forward and Zoe needed no second bidding. For the boxer, the monks' leftovers were on a par with the kind of thing his master gave him to eat. Zoe, though she hadn't ever realized it, had been pampered by her owners as far as her food was concerned, and she looked with misgiving at the vegetables, cheese and bread which lay in the dish. (The monks rarely ate meat.) Very gingerly, she began to eat. The bread and potatoes were edible, but she left the mash of carrots and peas in the dish, for Bertram to wolf down.

Bertram finished, licked all round his mouth and sighed. 'That's better,' he announced. Then he noticed Zoe's bowl wasn't empty. 'You're not going to leave that?' he asked.

'Yes, yes, I thought I would. You eat it if you really want it.'

Bertram didn't care if Zoe thought he was greedy. At his time of life he couldn't afford to be dainty and, besides, he had a much bigger body to fill. The vegetables disappeared.

Going to drink some water, Zoe's mind was filled with images of the raw mince and steak she had been used to eating at home. She was struck by a thought.

'I wonder if they'll come to look for me here,' she murmured to herself, and couldn't decide whether she wanted them to or not. Bertram rejoined her and lapped noisily and messily at the water-bowl. Zoe mentioned the thought to him, and he raised his head.

'Why ever should they come here?' he said at once. 'How could they possibly know we're on an island? No one else does.'

Zoe was silent. The full impact of what she had done hit her for the first time. What had seemed almost like a game to her was in reality much more serious. Fortunately, she wasn't able to think too long about the situation because Jack, who'd started the whole adventure, was calling them. 'Come on, come on,' he cried.

Now one of the mangy-looking cats was preparing to leave the courtyard. Hugging the wall, it crept round the square until it reached the arch. All the while it kept its eyes on the dogs. As soon as it reached the entrance it bolted, as if expecting them to give chase. Jack gave a couple of yaps just for form's sake, which startled the remaining cats more than the one who had disappeared.

'Let's leave,' Zoe said to Bertram. 'Jack's getting irritable.'

Bertram deliberately took another long drink to show Zoe that *he* wasn't at the beck and call of a mongrel. Then he condescended to go.

'The thing to remember,' Jack reminded them, 'is that you must come here the same time every day. Then you'll have nothing to worry about.'

'Where do we go now?' Zoe asked.

'Wherever you like. The whole island's yours to roam but, of course, you must guard against appearing in front of my master. He'd be bound to recognize you.'

'Oh yes, we mustn't do that,' Zoe pretended to agree. In reality she was much comforted by the thought of a possible escape route should she really need one.

'You must avoid the black and white house by the pool,' Jack explained. 'There's only one like it and it stands on its own. That's where we live.'

As they trotted through the archway a number of squirrels were gathering, running along the top of the wall in quick darts of movement. They came, as they always did, to see what remnants of food the larger animals had left.

Bertram said, 'We can avoid your master's house, but how do we avoid him? He doesn't stay at home all the time, does he?'

'No, of course not,' Jack replied. 'But if you see him, keep out of his way. You'd be certain to see him before he notices you: his eyes aren't too good. And, don't forget, he's not expecting to see you, is he? So you have all the advantages.'

The dogs were now leaving the monastery in the opposite direction from the one in which they had approached it. Their path soon took them into some thick woodland, where a soft carpet of the first fallen leaves smelt pungent and earthy under their paws. Zoe chased those drifting down in the still air, scattering clouds of others behind her. The scents and the warmth of the early-autumn day exhilarated her. Jack joined in her game and the two young dogs twisted and turned around the tree-trunks, tumbling each other over in the rustling bed of leaves. Bertram sighed and lay down against a fallen beech. He couldn't join in their sport and, having eaten well, was soon in a doze.

Suddenly, a pigeon clattered from a high branch and startled him into wakefulness. When he looked round he couldn't see Jack or Zoe anywhere. He cocked his head, listening hard for any barks, but there was nothing. Bertram wasn't anxious – only puzzled and rather jealous. He decided the two young dogs didn't want him around but enjoyed themselves more on their own. So why had he allowed himself to be dragged into this escapade? Then he recalled the kennels and how unhappy he had been in them; they were why he was here and he was glad of it. He got up, wondering if he should go in search of his companions, but he didn't need to. Zoe came bursting upon him through the trees, looking very upset.

'What—' Bertram began.

'Oh, thank goodness I found this place again,' Zoe cried. 'And you. Dear old Bertram. We – we – ,' she panted.

'Calm down, Zoe,' Bertram advised her. 'Get your breath back. You're quite safe. Now, what happened?'

'Jack and I were running,' Zoe went on after a bit. 'You know, playing. He ran off and hid himself somewhere; he's so much quicker on his legs than I am. I – I – couldn't find him anywhere. I searched all over and – and – then I got lost. I didn't know where I was or which way to go, so I panicked and started to follow a different path. It went round and round and up and up and' – she gulped – ' then I saw it!'

'Saw it? Saw what?'

'The giant!'

Bertram gaped. 'The – giant?'

'Yes, yes, I saw it, Bertram.'

'B-but,' spluttered the boxer, 'how do you know it was the giant – what you saw?'

'It must have been. It was huge. I've never seen—'

'Where was this?' demanded Bertram, trying to inject some confidence into his voice. 'What was it d-doing?'

'Nothing,' said Zoe. 'I didn't go close; I turned tail. But I'm sure it was just sitting. It was on the highest point, by a cliff-edge, and it seemed to be just gazing. Gazing out to sea.'

Bertram's alarm turned into anger now over Jack's irresponsibility. 'Fancy that careless mongrel vanishing like that!' he exclaimed. 'What a trick to play on you in a strange place!'

'I don't think he really meant to,' Zoe said honestly. 'He wouldn't do that. I just wasn't clever or quick enough to catch him.'

'You can't excuse him, Zoe,' Bertram insisted. 'It would never have happened if I'd been – if I'd – er—'

'Been awake?' Zoe suggested, archly.

'Oh, all right, I couldn't help it. I just felt drowsy,' Bertram said.

'Now you're excusing yourself,' Zoe pointed out.

'Yes, yes, I know. I suppose I'm partly to blame,' Bertram admitted. 'But where's Jack now?'

'I've got no idea where he is now. After I saw the giant I just fled. I tried to be calm and collected so that I could find my route back here, yet it was by luck alone, I'm sure, that I found you again.'

'Well, now you have found me, I think we should move on,' said Bertram. 'Despite everything, I'm rather intrigued by this giant business. Could you find it again, d'you think? I'd like to investigate.'

'You *mean* it?' Zoe gasped. 'You really want me to—'

'Of course,' Bertram assured her, feeling terribly brave. 'You mustn't risk yourself, though; you just point me in the right direction, d'you see?'

'All right, I'll try,' Zoe said. 'What about Jack?'

'What about him? He knows the island. I'm sure he can find us if he wants.'

'Yes. That's true. I wonder what he's up to?'

Considerably calmed, as usual, by Bertram's presence, Zoe was able to follow the paths rather more clear-headedly this time. Eventually she found the winding one that climbed up the headland, and stopped by a lone rowan tree standing at the far boundary of the wood.

'I'll wait here,' said the little terrier. 'Just keep going on this path and – and – you'll see it.'

'If it's still there,' Bertram added. 'Don't start fretting, now,' he said kindly. 'I shan't be long.'

Zoe watched his brindled body heaving up the steep path, his bandy legs treading carefully. Every so often he paused to look around and to recover his wheezing breath. Then a sharp curve hid him from view.

Bertram plodded on. Just as the land dropped away to his right, giving him sight of the broad sweep of surrounding sea, he spied a great still figure up ahead at the end of the path, seated on a sort of pinnacle, and placidly gazing out across the water. Bertram dropped to his belly, flattening himself against the stony track. The head of the giant was turning his way.

7

The Island Dog

When Bertram dared to raise himself again he did so very slowly and very cautiously. He found the giant sitting as before, silhouetted against the sun and the sky, its head once more focussed seaward. Bertram didn't go any closer. He backtracked and met Zoe by the rowan tree.

The terrier danced out at him, crying excitedly, 'Did you see it? Isn't it absolutely huge?'

'Yes, I saw it,' he said, pretending to be unimpressed. 'It's big all right, but not *that* big.'

'Oh, you don't fool me!' Zoe countered. 'You've come back rather quickly, I notice. Admit it, Bertram, you've never seen such a beast.'

'I didn't get quite close enough to make sure of that,' he told her. 'And actually—' He broke off. 'Why, here's Jack!' The mongrel was hovering at the edge of the woods.

'Wherever have you been?' Zoe snapped at him. 'You got me lost! I didn't know where to go.'

'What are you doing up here?' Jack demanded. 'You should keep away from these parts, it's not safe. Humans don't venture along this path. The ground crumbles at times and—'

'I saw the giant!' Zoe announced importantly. 'I

brought Bertram to see.' She and Bertram meanwhile returned to the cover of the trees.

'Ah – you've seen him,' Jack answered flatly. He sounded a little disappointed, as if he had been saving up the island's main attraction to show to them personally and had now been cheated of the pleasure.

'Tell us about him,' Zoe urged, as they rustled through the leaves.

'Oh, he's always there in the daytime,' Jack replied. 'In the same spot, every day. Always looking, looking; constantly looking out to sea.'

'What's it – he – looking *for*?' inquired Zoe.

'No one knows. He's been waiting for something for ever.'

'How strange,' grunted Bertram. 'And does he stay there all night too?'

'No one knows where he goes at night,' Jack said mysteriously.

'But there are people on this island. Your master, the Good People. Surely they—' Bertram continued, but Jack cut him short.

'As I said, humans don't go up there,' he reminded him. 'They don't care to. There were accidents. . . .'

'Unsafe,' Zoe repeated to the boxer.

'Yes, dangerous,' Jack underlined. 'In heavy rain, there are sometimes cliff falls. Rocks, soil – swept away.'

'But the Giant sits on, of course,' Bertram said, sarcastically.

'So it would seem,' Jack said, not in the least disconcerted. 'He's still there, isn't he?'

'Where could he have come from?' Zoe murmured. She was fascinated by this mystery.

Bertram was interested, too, though he wouldn't have admitted it to Jack. He made up his mind to have a

second look some time on his own, danger or no danger.
But he meant to keep this from Zoe. He didn't want her
following him and neither did he want the mongrel's
company. So he decided to make a pretence of being
sleepy, in the hope that they would leave him to go gam-
bolling off somewhere. That would be his opportunity.
He slowed up and began to fall behind. As usual Jack and
Zoe raced on ahead, chattering busily and not immediately
noticing his absence. When Zoe did at last turn, she saw
that Bertram was lying comfortably on his side in a thick
pile of leaves. 'Oh look, Jack!' she exclaimed. 'I do
believe Bertram's gone to sleep again.'

'Let him,' was the mongrel's reply, 'if that's what he
wants. He's old. Let's go down to the beach; I know a
quiet place where the sand is hard and flat – wonderful to
run on. We'll know where to find the old fellow when we
come back.'

Bertram's plan had worked. He waited a while until
the two youngsters were out of sight and then he pulled
himself back on to his feet, gave his body a good shake to
get rid of the leaves and twigs, and unhurriedly made off
towards the rising path again.

This time he went with more confidence. There was no
young female terrier to watch how he went. He reached
the rowan tree once more at the wood's edge and then
proceeded more cautiously up the steep rise. The giant
was, amazingly, still at the same point and in the same
position. Bertram had only seen the figure from the back
before; this time he went farther along the path and, as it
curved round a rock, he saw the creture for the first time
from the side. Getting himself on the other side of the
rock, Bertram peered round and took a long look. The
giant was a dog just as he was and just as he had suspected.
It was huge, but a dog nonetheless. Under the rough,
matted grey hair, its body was lean. It was immensely tall,

with a long, slender tail and a bony head with powerful jaws. Yet it seemed so lonely to Bertram, sitting in this isolated spot, that he felt a twinge of sympathy for it and was not in the least overawed. He recognized the animal as a wolfhound. Deciding not to approach the great dog, he watched it for a long time. For most of that time it was motionless. Then a shift in the direction of the autumn breeze carried Bertram's scent up to the giant and it began to snuffle the air. Bertram judged it was time to retreat and he turned back along the path once more. However, the wolfhound appeared to have little interest in the intruder and, although Bertram didn't see this, merely looked round and followed him for a while with its eyes.

The old boxer went looking for Zoe. He wanted to reassure her about the giant and also to put himself one up against Jack, who didn't seem to know what the creature was. He easily found them on the beach, guided by their high-spirited cries. The wood ran almost clear down to the shore, and then he turned to the right over the turf and went on to the sand. Jack was racing about, snapping up bits of driftwood and tossing them into the air, then dashing off after some other object. Zoe couldn't match his speed and was watching him with admiration, occasionally whining as if she wished she could join in. Bertram glowered at the spectacle – he knew perfectly well Jack was just showing off.

'He'll wear himself out if he carries on like that,' the boxer muttered.

Zoe glanced up. 'There you are,' she said. 'Been dozing again?'

'Not at all,' Bertram returned. 'I've been back to the cliff and found out all about this wonderful giant.' He sounded contemptuous.

'*Have* you?' Zoe was astonished and took her eyes off

Jack's antics to look at the old boxer properly. 'What have you discovered then?'

Bertram looked back into her bright eager eyes. 'Oh – he's just a dog like all of us. A wolfhound actually.'

'That sounds fierce.'

'Well, he certainly isn't,' Bertram told her. 'He never moves. Just stares and stares. I could have gone right up to him, but I thought I should come and join you or you'd be worrying where I was.'

Zoe looked guilty, as he had meant her to. 'Er – well, really, we hadn't started to get worried. We were going to come back for you, you see.'

Jack had paused. He had noticed he no longer had an audience and he stood far out on the sand, his sides heaving from his exertions, watching the other two. Then he came towards them. 'Tell Jack about the wolfhound,' Zoe prompted.

'I shall.'

'Glad you found us all right,' were Jack's first words. 'We thought it best not to disturb you.'

Bertram was irritated by what he took to be the young's condescending attitude towards the old. 'Don't think I spend all my time sleeping,' he snapped, forgetting that he had deliberately pretended to be asleep to shake off the mongrel. 'No, I've been investigating your famous giant. Haven't you realized it's merely a wolfhound?'

Jack looked a little uncomfortable. Not for the first time, he felt that Bertram disliked him. 'A wolfhound?' he repeated. 'Oh, he may well be. What of it?'

'Well, he's just a dog like ourselves. Nothing to be scared of,' Bertram continued with a superior air.

'Who said anything about being scared?' Jack defended himself. '*I'm* not scared.'

'No? That's good,' Bertram wheezed. 'You've spoken to the poor solitary creature then, have you?'

'Spoken? Well – er, no, not actually spoken, not exactly. Of course I'm very familiar with the sight of him. He's been there as long as I can remember.'

'And that's all you know about the great giant? Well, well, we shall have to try and discover a bit more about him, won't we, Zoe?' Bertram said, looking at her as if they were in a kind of partnership.

Jack looked a bit crestfallen. Before he could try to re-assert himself, Bertram said, 'I knew a wolfhound once. There used to be one on the beach, a fisherman's dog. I don't know what happened to it or its owner – they haven't been seen around for a long while. But I always remember one thing about that dog. It had the habit of howling every time the church bells rang. I suppose it didn't like the sound.'

Jack gave an involuntary start, but he said nothing more about the wolfhound. 'Do you want me to show you more of the island?' he asked abruptly.

'Oh yes,' said Zoe at once. 'We must get to know our way around, mustn't we, Bertram?'

'Oh – if you like,' the old boxer answered, without much interest. 'But don't you and Jack go charging off like two puppies. Try to remember my pace, or I may as well stay behind.'

'Of course we'll remember,' Jack said. 'But if you'd rather not, don't feel you have to come. I don't want to tire you out.'

Bertram was determined not to be left out. 'I'm coming,' he declared flatly.

They followed the beach round past the mouth of the small gully where, farther up, the little wood grew. They were moving away from the spot where Bertram and Zoe had first swum ashore. Now the cliffs reached right down to the strand and in many places the rock had been hollowed out into caves that just invited exploration. Zoe was a little wary, however. 'What's in them? They're so dark. Have you been inside them, Jack?'

'Well, Zoe, what do you think? This is my home territory, all of this. I know each and every one.'

'My!'

'Pooh, there's nothing to be frightened of there,' Bertram scoffed. 'Only, if I know caves, they'll all be uncomfortably damp and slippery and dripping with water.'

'Old pessimist,' commented Zoe good-humouredly. She ran after Jack who was already deep into one cavern.

'Oooh, this is fun,' her echoing barks came from inside. 'Bertram, this one's quite dry.'

Bertram clambered laboriously over the stones and boulders that littered the mouth of the cave. Some of them were beautifully smooth and shiny, others were encrusted with barnacles and limpets. Once or twice he stumbled. He saw no fun in it at all, but Jack and Zoe were waiting for him, so he had to go on.

'This cave,' Jack announced when Bertram joined them, 'always stays dry. It's worth remembering: you may need it.'

'Need it?' Bertram muttered to Zoe. 'Surely he doesn't think we're going to become cave dwellers?'

'No, no,' she whispered hastily. 'Just for shelter – you know, from rain.'

Bertram hadn't planned to spend any of his time in dark caves. 'It wouldn't be very comfortable,' he observed to Jack, 'if we needed a long spell here. All those cold hard stones lying about.'

'Well, we must hope it won't be necessary,' said the mongrel. 'But you could always drag some softer bedding in – grass and leaves and so on, couldn't you?'

'Grass and leaves!' retorted Bertram. 'From a beach?'

'I'd help,' Jack offered.

Farther round, the beach ended in a wall of rock. Jack led them up a steep path through thick grass which skirted the rock face and brought them round above it. A stream ran over a pebbly bed at breakneck speed, downhill to the sea. The three dogs were now very high up, on the other side of the little island from the wolfhound's vantage point.

'I can get home in this direction,' Jack announced. 'It's a long way round, but it goes through a farm which I like to visit. I have a friend there.'

'Oh,' said Zoe. 'What – er – what sort of a friend?'

Bertram noticed with amusement that she sounded a little put out.

'Come and see for yourself, if you like,' Jack suggested. 'But you mustn't go beyond the farm because you'd be getting a bit too close to my master's house.'

'How far is it?' Bertram wanted to know. He wasn't the slightest bit interested in Jack's friend.

'Not too far,' Jack answered.

'Hm! That tells me a lot,' the boxer grumbled and, rather pointedly, sat on his haunches. His big, blunt muzzle jutted forward in a typically obstinate way. Zoe could tell at once he didn't want to go but, for reasons of her own, she was rather eager to find out about this 'friend'.

'Here we go again,' she complained. 'Bertram, why are you squatting there like that? You said you wanted to see the island.'

'I've seen plenty of it already,' he answered. 'Can't we have a rest? Climbing all the way up here has winded me.'

'We couldn't have come much more slowly,' Zoe replied. 'You're always wanting a rest or a nap or something.'

'Wait till you're my age,' Bertram muttered for the umpteenth time. It was one of his favourite responses. 'Never mind me, Zoe. You go on and I'll catch you up after a bit.'

Zoe looked from the old boxer to Jack, who was prancing about, keen to be moving again. She felt torn between the two.

'Go on, Zoe,' Bertram repeated. 'I'll come later. Do I stick to this path?'

'The very same,' said Jack and he bounded off without further hesitation, as if he had just been released from a chain.

'I'll wait for you,' Zoe promised as she ran after him.

Bertram watched them disappear. Alone, he became aware of a strange sense of emptiness in his surroundings. For a while he couldn't think what the reason was, then all at once he realized. It was the total lack of human beings.

Since early morning, when one of the Good People had brought food, there had been no people visible anywhere. To Bertram, the contrast with Multon, where he was used to seeing seaside crowds, was very marked. The island was so quiet and – yes, empty. As he pondered over this, all at once he plainly heard the bells of the monastery church ringing. The insistent clangour carried easily to every point of the island. Although he didn't understand what the ringing was for, Bertram was reminded of a similar sound he had been used to hearing at intervals on the mainland. Then the bells were followed by another sound which wafted across to him from the heights, and really made the boxer's ears prick up. It was an eerie, hollow howling, so mournful that his flesh crawled. But Bertram knew what it was. For him, at least part of the mystery of the giant was solved.

8

A Clue and a Riddle

After a short rest, Bertram plodded off in the direction the younger dogs had taken. He didn't want to keep his discovery to himself any longer. Meanwhile Jack and Zoe, who hadn't stopped running, were approaching the farm.

The dying bracken which had almost overgrown the narrow path all along gave way to more open terrain and there, on the right-hand side ahead of them, were all the buildings and pens of a little farm. Zoe's nostrils picked up a heady mixture of pungent smells that were new to her, among them that of the warm bodies of animals. She was excited, but wary. Jack led her by the side of a long stretch of fencing to a little gate. He pulled himself through a gap underneath into the yard, expecting Zoe to follow him, but she hesitated nervously.

'Come on,' he encouraged her. 'Nothing to be afraid of here.'

'No, no, I'll, er, wait here,' she answered. 'I don't know this place and – and – nobody knows me, do they?'

'It's all right, I tell you,' Jack said. But he could see she wouldn't budge so he ran on, around the corner of the farmhouse. Zoe assumed he was seeking his friend.

Washing flapped on a line in the garden and a cow mooed loudly from a field, startling Zoe momentarily, but there was neither sign nor sound of people, nor of the dog Zoe was expecting to see. Then she heard Jack barking by the house, announcing himself, and human voices answering him. A door opened and a chortling, high-pitched voice full of glee rose above the others. Zoe saw Jack returning towards the gate, chased by a delighted little blonde girl about three years old, carefully wrapped in woollens, who continually chanted, 'Here's Jack! Here's Jack!'

The mongrel spun round and round in his sporty way, keeping the girl in sight and bringing her towards Zoe. 'Here's my playmate!' he cried to the terrier. 'She loves to run after me. Come and join in the fun!'

The little girl hadn't yet noticed Zoe peering under the gate. She was clutching a rubber ball which she now threw in a small child's stiff way at Jack. He took one of his elastic leaps, caught the ball in his jaws and raced off round the other side of the house. The girl shrieked her pleasure and ran after him in hot pursuit. Zoe wagged her stump of a tail unconsciously, longing to be in this game. As Jack came round again, having made a circuit of the house, he juggled and snapped at the ball. The little girl's legs were no match for the dog's speed and she had lost sight of him.

'Where are you? Where are you?' she cried. 'Jack, Jack, come back!'

Zoe could resist no longer. She squirmed under the gate, straight into the path of the little girl, who squealed even louder at having a second dog to play with. Her mother emerged from the house.

'Who have we here?' she said in surprise. 'What a lovely clean little dog. As white as snow!' Her tone was so warm and kindly that Zoe wagged her tail and felt no fear of her. Then she set off after Jack, soon taking the ball from him and chasing it along the ground.

The girl's shrieks and the dogs' excited barks could be

heard by Bertram as he blundered on through the bracken. The boxer wondered what was going on. Eventually he reached the farm and the gate. Getting on to his hind legs and resting his front half on the gate-top, he looked with amazement at the sight that greeted his eyes. A plump round-faced little girl, no taller than Bertram as he stood then, was rushing about between the two dogs as they circled round and round. Her blue eyes were wide with enjoyment and her cheeks flushed with exercise. They were all so involved in their game with the ball that none of them noticed Bertram, and the girl's mother was attending to the washing.

'Zoe! Jack! I've something to tell you,' Bertram called.

They were unheeding, scarcely hearing him. Only the little girl took notice of his breathy barks and came trotting over. She put out a tentative hand very slowly and patted his wrinkled head. Bertram gulped: he wasn't used to human caresses. He licked her hand with his rather slobbery tongue, but the little girl didn't mind it a bit and called to her mother, 'Mummy, look, another one!'

'Where *are* all these dogs coming from all of a sudden?' her mother asked herself.

Now Jack and Zoe saw the game was finished for a while. Zoe made straight for the gate and wriggled through to join Bertram, while Jack stayed on the other side with an air of greater familiarity, as if he belonged there.

Bertram dropped back on all fours. 'Did you hear the bells?' he asked Zoe.

She looked puzzled. 'Bells? Oh yes. I think so.'

'Well,' Bertram added impatiently, 'didn't you notice anything?'

'What do you mean?'

'Come away from here, and I'll explain all about it.'

They moved farther down the path. Jack scurried after them. 'Don't go too far,' he reminded them. 'My master sometimes walks up this way.'

'Well, Bertram, what is it?' Zoe prompted.

'The wolfhound,' he said. 'I think he's the same one that I knew at home. If so, he must have been here a long, long time; I can't remember when I last saw him on the beach.' He explained about the howling.

'Well, what of it?' Jack asked, as if he wasn't particularly interested.

'There's a mystery, isn't there? How did he get here?'

'I told *you* there was a mystery,' said Jack.

'But don't you want to solve it?'

'Oh yes,' Zoe interrupted. 'I do. I do.'

'Come on then, what are we waiting for?' Bertram said.

'I'm close to home now,' said Jack awkwardly. 'I think I'll go on. I like to show myself on and off during the day. My master likes that. I'll, er, see you later?'

'Up to you,' Bertram answered. He was secretly glad to have Zoe to himself for a while. Zoe looked disappointed but she let Jack go.

'D'you know,' said Bertram, 'I do believe our friend is a little frightened of his "giant".'

'Oh no,' Zoe replied at once. 'I don't think *he's* frightened of anything.'

'You always defend him, don't you?' grumbled Bertram. 'I wonder if you'd defend me if he—'

'Oh shut up, Bertram,' she barked. 'Don't be so boring.'

'But would you?'

'Well – yes.'

Bertram was satisfied.

They set off, back through the rusty bracken. Zoe headed down to the beach.

'Why go that way again?' queried Bertram. 'Perhaps there's a high path straight across to the giant's pinnacle.'

'I see. I didn't know you were planning to confront him.'

'How else can we discover his secret?'

Zoe was still in awe of the Great Dog she had only glimpsed from a distance, and dithered a little. 'But we don't know any other path,' she said. 'If we don't go back down to the beach and then up through the wood, we may get lost.'

'I don't think so,' said Bertram confidently. 'Leave it to me.'

So, when the path started to dip down they ignored it and continued straight on across the cliff tops. Bertram was proved right, for it wasn't long before they joined up with the path they had found earlier, which led to the wolfhound's lookout.

'You *are* clever,' Zoe said admiringly.

'Just common sense,' Bertram told her. 'My pace may be slow, but this is such a small island, every place is close to another.'

Zoe didn't question this rather mysterious remark, but when she spied the huge silhouette in its usual spot, she began to hang back. Bertram understood her fear. 'Don't worry,' he said kindly. 'I'll go first and when I'm sure of him I'll call you.' He turned and looked at the little terrier. 'And if I don't call,' he added, 'you stay put.'

Zoe promptly sat down and licked her chops nervously; Bertram went ahead. The giant didn't move a muscle as the boxer approached. Bertram couldn't be sure if he detected his presence or not. At last, treading carefully because of Jack's warning about the unsafe ground, he drew level and sat beside the wolfhound, following his gaze out to sea in an effort to see what he was looking at. For along time neither dog said anything. At last Bertram broke the silence.

'Are you waiting for something?' he asked in a low voice.

There was no answer.

'Or – someone?'

Finally the wolfhound turned his head to look at him. Below his chin there was a diamond-shaped patch of white hair which contrasted noticeably with the great mass of grey which covered the rest of his body. Bertram recognized it at once and knew beyond doubt this was the same dog he used to see long ago in Multon.

The wolfhound opened his great jaws. In a very deep, gruff voice he said, 'Why do you question me?'

'I, er, I'm interested,' Bertram answered lamely, and then quickly added, 'I know you.'

'You know me? No one knows me here.'

'*I* do. I used to see you in earlier days, back home. On shore.'

The wolfhound gave a barely perceptible start, but it was enough to tell Bertram he was right. 'You belonged to a fisherman, didn't you?'

'Yes.'

'Is that who you're watching for, day after day, up here?'

The wolfhound didn't answer directly. 'I know he'll come. Sometime,' he said. 'He must do.' His deep voice conveyed immeasurable sadness, and the look in his eyes when he stared at Bertram reflected it too. Bertram trembled. He felt himself powerfully affected by such overwhelming emotion.

'Won't you tell me about him?' he asked gently. 'Why did he abandon you?'

'He didn't!' the great dog cried with a fierce loyalty. 'I'm not abandoned. Only – separated.'

Bertram waited for him to go on, but when no more information seemed forthcoming, tried a new approach: one of friendliness.

'Do you have a name?' he enquired. 'I'm called Bertram.'

'I'm Liam,' the wolfhound answered simply, turning his gaze once more out to sea.

Bertram asked, 'Is that where you were separated from – from your master? Out there?'

Liam sighed. There was a long silence. Bertram was on the point of speaking again, when suddenly the wolfhound said, in a low voice, 'It was a storm, you see. We were in the boat. There were enormous waves, and we got beaten and battered. Then the boat turned over. I tried to swim, but I couldn't see anything. I was hurled about and in the end, with a bit of help, I was swept on to this island. I lay on the beach for a long time, thinking I could never move again, but I forced myself up at last. I knew I had to wait, to hold on for my master.'

'And,' Bertram whispered, 'you are still waiting?'

'Yes. I must wait here. He'll come one day. He'll know where I am.'

Bertram was silent – he felt certain the fisherman must have drowned. In Multon he had disappeared from sight at the same time as his dog. But it seemed the wolfhound had great faith. . . .

At last the boxer said, almost without thinking, 'Suppose he came at night? You wouldn't see him.'

Liam said, 'My master will only come to this island for one reason: to seek his dog, old Liam. So he wouldn't come in the dark.'

'Where do you go at night?' Bertram asked.

'Where do *you* go?' Liam returned, but before Bertram

could answer, he added mysteriously, 'I eat at night.'

'At night?' Bertram exclaimed. 'But how? Surely the Good People don't—'

The great dog interrupted. 'I have nothing to do with people.'

Bertram was baffled. 'Then what . . . ? How . . . ?'

'I'll say no more,' the wolfhound told him. 'I didn't ask you to come questioning me.'

Bertram knew there was no arguing with that tone. He got up and wandered away, his mind busy with a new riddle. Suddenly, he remembered Zoe had been waiting all along for his call and hurried back to her. 'Oh Bertram, I'm so relieved,' she greeted him. 'I've been so concerned about you. I heard nothing and I thought—'

'I had come to harm?' he suggested. 'Don't worry, Zoe, I've returned unhurt. But I'm glad you care enough to worry about me,' he finished mischievously.

'Of course I do. With that great beast sitting up there. . . .'

'Liam? I don't think he'd do me any harm.'

'So you spoke to him then?'

'Yes. How did you know that?'

'How else would you know his name, you silly old dog?' Zoe barked impatiently.

'I was forgetting,' he replied. 'But he only spoke when I urged him. He told me a bit about himself: I know how he got here, and I know he's the same animal I used to see, ages ago. I recognized him at close quarters. There's still a mystery though, Zoe. How does he eat? What can he find at *night*?'

Zoe shuddered. 'I – I – don't know,' she whispered. Her hackles rose in spite of herself.

'Does he hunt other creatures, like a fox does? But what kind of creatures?'

'Oh Bertram, let's go. I don't like it up here,' Zoe wailed. She was frightened. 'I don't like this great dog who's so strange and – and – unknown,' she added, for want of a better word. 'Supposing he does "hunt", as you say. Where could we hide from him?'

Bertram realized he had scared her, and hastened to offer reassurance. 'Poor Zoe, don't be so alarmed,' he soothed. 'You've nothing to fear; dog doesn't eat dog. Perhaps he finds mice or . . . or . . . oh, I don't know what there is to hunt. I don't understand it, I'm not a hunting animal. I only know wild creatures have to find their own food.'

Zoe said, 'Is he – a wild – creature?' She still hadn't recovered her composure.

'No, no, he was a pet, like us. A fisherman's dog. Let me explain.' And Bertram told the terrier all that the wolfhound had told him.

When he had finished Zoe said compassionately, 'It's a sad story.' They found themselves re-entering the little wood, having walked on without really thinking about where they were going. 'Where are we heading for?' she asked the boxer.

Bertram paused and looked about him, as if realizing for the first time exactly where they were. 'D'you know, Zoe,' he said, 'I haven't the faintest idea. I've never been in this situation before. We can go anywhere, do anything. It's strange, isn't it? And the strangest thing of all is I simply don't know where to go next.'

'Do we have to go anywhere?' she queried. 'Perhaps we should stay where Jack can find us again.'

Bertram didn't want to listen to anything about Jack. 'It's important,' he said, 'we should have a headquarters, a – a – base. You know, like at home. Now where would the best place be?'

'What about that cave Jack showed us?'

'Certainly not,' Bertram retorted immediately without even considering it. 'The place has to be comfortable and homely. In fact, what's wrong with somewhere here?

Plenty of leaves to curl up in.'

'It's too open,' said Zoe. 'Any other creature could come wandering through here.' She was still thinking of Liam. 'Actually,' she went on, 'I can't think of anywhere better than where we first slept after we swam ashore. It was a good place to rest undisturbed.'

'All right,' Bertram agreed, forgetting for the moment Jack had introduced them to that spot too. 'Would you know how to find it again?'

'It's back near the jetty where the boat came in,' said Zoe. 'If we go to the beach it must be the opposite way from the route we took to the caves.'

'I think you're right,' said Bertram.

And she was. The only problem was that once they got down on the beach, farther round in that direction the tide now covered the sand. However they found they could push their way through the vegetation up the slopes and work their path round that way. Soon Bertram picked up Zoe's old scent and Zoe detected Bertram's, leading to a hollowed-out patch of rough grass and bracken amongst the scrub. Some snowy white hairs showed the exact place where Zoe had slept the previous night.

'It seems so long ago since we were here last,' she remarked. 'And yet it hasn't been.'

They made themselves comfortable. 'I wonder if we'll see Jack again today,' Zoe murmured.

'You wonder a lot about him,' said Bertram pointedly and yawned widely. 'What I wonder is – why was he so keen for us to come here in the first place?'

'Haven't you worked that out yet?' Zoe replied. 'He's lonely. There are no other dogs here so far as I can see, apart from one whom I shan't count. Jack wanted company.'

'I might have known it would be a selfish motive,' Bertram muttered.

9

A Strange Partnership

Zoe and Bertram saw no more of Jack that day. At dusk Zoe fell asleep. She'd felt hungry, as she'd been used to eating twice a day; food figured largely in her dreams. Bertram lay awake, but not because he was hungry. He wasn't used to a second meal and in any case wasn't uncomfortable because he'd eaten much more than Zoe at the monastery. He couldn't stop thinking about Liam. Where would the wolfhound be now that it was dark? He would be looking for food, but what food and where? Bertram wondered if he dare go in search of him, he was so brimful of curiosity. But then he thought of Zoe. If she should wake and find herself alone she'd be scared, so he decided to stay put.

In the morning Jack redeemed himself in Bertram's eyes when he arrived on the scene very early to rouse them for feeding time.

'You see,' Zoe whispered to Bertram, 'he's not entirely selfish.' And the boxer couldn't help but agree.

'You'll get used to the time yourselves soon, or your stomachs will,' Jack quipped. 'You won't need me to wake you.'

They made their way along the route they had taken on the previous day towards the Good People's place. Bertram did his best to memorize it as they went.

'You found us easily,' Zoe remarked to Jack.

'Yes, I'm glad I tried that spot first. I thought it likely you'd be there. Is that to be your regular sleeping quarters?'

'Yes, I think so. Isn't it, Bertram?'

'Yes. Listen, Jack, I've found out more about our giant. Do you want to hear?'

'Of course – if you think it of interest,' Jack answered diffidently.

'Very much of interest,' Bertram assured him and told him what he had discovered.

'I guessed it was something like that,' Jack remarked, only half-truthfully.

'Do you want to find out more?' Bertram asked. He was hoping Jack would go with him to learn where Liam went at night. Then Zoe couldn't help but follow.

'You're *very* concerned about him, aren't you?' Jack commented. 'I feel he might prefer to be left alone.'

'Maybe. But surely, you can't just ignore a secret like that on your own home island?'

Jack was stumped for a reply. He certainly didn't want Bertram, a much older, slower animal, to be the one with all the initiative. 'All right,' he said, making it sound as if he were just trying to keep Bertram happy, 'we'll go tonight.'

They reached the entrance to the monastery court-yard, where the mangy cats were pacing along one wall and then back like caged animals. Again they looked at the dogs very nervously and, seeing how timid they were, Bertram suddenly wondered if it were animals such as these that Liam hunted in the dark. But the cats' lithe, agile movements made it unlikely they could be caught with ease. They seemed excited. The dogs discovered they had caught the smell of fish which soon appeared, mixed in with other ingredients, in the food bowls.

The robed human stood a while to watch them eat. He

then conscientiously filled the water-bowls and, as he disappeared, the squirrels gathered to select their titbits from the larger animals' leavings. Zoe and Bertram both made a hearty meal, for the little dog had decided she would have to stop being fussy.

'I do believe you get more to eat here than my master gives me,' Jack observed.

'But *you* get meat, no doubt,' Bertram reminded him.

'Yes. And perhaps you'll find some here one day.'

'D'you think so?' Zoe said. 'Then we *should* want for nothing.'

Bertram wasn't so sure about that. But it was another beautiful day, the sun shone warmly, a breeze blew fresh, tangy scents in from the sea, and they could do whatever they liked, so any objections were easily forgotten. The three dogs spent some hours romping on the beach – even the old boxer felt lighthearted enough to try to join in for a while – then they lay in the sun and dozed, which suited him better. Later Jack suggested he show them the remainder of the island but, as there wasn't anything particularly interesting in that quarter, Zoe and Bertram were not keen.

'What is there to see?' Zoe asked.

'Cliffs, thick ferns, a little stream. . . .' Jack answered.

'Very much like this side,' remarked Bertram and yawned.

'There is something I'd like to see,' said Zoe.

'Yes? What?' Jack looked lively again, after his disappointment.

'Your home.'

'Oh – you know you can't.'

'Doesn't your master ever leave it?'

'Of course he does. He has to go and get our food from the shop and – well, sometimes he visits other people.

'Couldn't we come when he's not there?'

'How do I know his plans? Besides, if I'm around he takes me with him.'

Jack eventually left them, to 'put in an appearance' as he phrased it, promising to return before dusk. Bertram was impatient for darkness, but Zoe had no enthusiasm at all for the evening's trek. She knew she must go or be left by herself, and that was unthinkable.

Jack returned in good time and they set off silently for the wood. Under the trees it already seemed dark to Zoe, but when they emerged on to the little climbing path, there was still plenty of daylight left. Bertram was eager to be near Liam's look-out before he left his post so that they could follow him when he did move. 'You seem more sprightly,' Jack remarked, noticing the Boxer's unusual speed.

'I shall pay for this, I expect,' Bertram answered and in fact, his breath was already labouring.

'Don't overdo it, Bertram,' Zoe said kindly. *She* didn't want to follow the great, grey dog.

None of them spoke again for a time. Then Bertram wheezed, 'Good. He's still there.'

Although the other two didn't know it, Jack was actually closer to the wolfhound than he had ever been before and, certainly, not without qualms. The giant's body was so perfectly still – a dark shape against the darkening horizon – and it seemed they would never discover the animal's strange secrets. Only Bertram went forward with confidence. Just out of earshot of the giant, he made the others sink down with him behind a rock, keeping just enough in view to see when the day's watch was over. Not until the thickening gloom had wrapped the whole island round did the wolfhound stir. Bertram detected movement but, when he stood up, the great dog appeared to have melted into the darkness. There was no trace of him.

'Quickly, follow me,' the boxer ordered. He shambled towards the pinnacle where Liam always sat, the others keeping well behind. Jack knew best of all about the dangers of the cliff edge.

'Careful, Bertram,' he cautioned the boxer, who was casting about, this way and that, for a sign.

'I can smell him,' he declared with frustration. 'Where can he have gone? There's no path here.'

'There's certainly no path,' Jack agreed, 'except one through the air which would be the last any of us would ever take.'

Bertram seemed all at once to recognize the danger and drew back. 'But where . . . ,' he muttered and sniffed hard at the ground, 'where on earth could he. . . .' He suddenly gave a bark of triumph which terrified Zoe and made Jack jump in the air.

'There!' Bertram cried. 'I see it! There *is* a path – through the rock!'

Jack and Zoe ran up to him and, with some difficulty in the darkness, discovered a gap in the bare rock close to where Liam had been sitting. It took them a while to make out that there was a passage leading off this gap like a sort of rocky tunnel.

'That's where he's gone – down there,' Bertram said. 'There's just no other way.'

Jack didn't know anything about this passageway. 'Humans must have made it,' he said, 'but none use it now, *I* know. They never come to these parts.'

'No. Only Liam knows of it,' Bertram said. 'Except *we* know it now, too. Come on, let's follow him.'

'Oh no,' Zoe whined. 'I don't want to go in there. Please, Bertram, let's stay away.'

The boxer ignored her; he was too excited to pull back now. 'What about you?' he asked Jack.

Jack had no more desire to go into the rock tunnel than Zoe, but he couldn't admit that. 'I'm game,' he lied, 'though we can't leave Zoe on this side on her own.'

Bertram was determined not to be put off. 'Oh, she'll be all right. Liam's vanished and you said yourself no one else ever comes up here.'

Jack couldn't think of a reply to that. So he said, 'Just a brief look, then, to satisfy your curiosity, and straight back here.'

Bertram entered the passage without another word, Jack behind him reluctantly. Zoe trembled at the entrance, not knowing whether to stay or go along for the sake of companionship. The tunnel curved and she saw Jack's hind legs disappear from view. For a few moments she could still hear paws pattering on the rock floor, then there was silence. 'Oh dear,' she wailed to herself, 'what shall I do?' She wildly imagined Liam's huge shape suddenly looming up from behind, materializing from some other secret path. Her little body began to shake uncontrollably and, in desperation, she dived into the hole and ran after the others.

Bertram found that the passage ahead widened and dipped down more and more sharply, until he had difficulty in preventing his paws sliding. The rock floor, however, was uneven and pitted, which helped him and Jack to maintain their grip. Eventually the deep blackness of the passage gave way to another opening where there was slightly more light. Bertram stepped out into a lofty, arched cave. He could see, some distance ahead, a stretch of sand and beyond it the murmuring sea. He halted so abruptly that Jack bumped into him.

'Look,' Bertram whispered hoarsely. 'We're back by the beach.'

'Not any beach I know,' said the mongrel. 'I've never been here before.'

There was still no sign of the wolfhound. Just as they were deciding to explore the cave, Zoe came scrabbling down the end of the passage. The three dogs moved forward together. The cave opened out into a secluded cove, with a short, crescent-shaped area of sand littered with fallen boulders from the cliffs above. It was enclosed on three sides by sheer walls of dark granite. At the mouth of the cave was an assortment of human debris – scraps of clothing, a sea-boot and a broken tobacco pipe. Jack recognized this because it was like something his master used, but none of the animals paid the pile of oddments much attention.

It was Zoe who spotted the wolfhound. He was at the far right-hand side of the cove and he was standing in the water, so deep that the ripples reached his chin. She could see this quite clearly by the light of a full moon.

'Whatever is he doing?' she asked.

Bertram was keen to investigate, but Jack, and Zoe in particular, preferred to watch proceedings from where they stood.

Jack suddenly yapped, 'There's another animal, look! Farther out, actually swimming up and down.'

Bertram strained his eyes but couldn't see anything except the wavelets running inshore. Zoe saw though, and her fur rose.

'It's – it's – not a dog. It's a strange animal,' she whimpered, drawn to the sight despite her timidity. 'You can see its head above the water. It's swimming up and down with a – a – wiggly movement.'

'Like a great fish,' Jack commented, in an awe-struck tone.

'Where? Where?' Bertram demanded in exasperation.

'I can't see it.'

'The giant's watching it,' Zoe told him. 'He seems to be waiting for it in some way.'

The strange animal rose more out of the water, looking directly at Liam, then plunged back under the waves. But Jack had seen enough now to identify it. 'It's a seal,' he said, with an evident note of relief in his voice. 'You often see them around the island. Sometimes they come ashore and lie about.'

The other two had never seen such a beast, but Zoe was comforted by Jack's reassurance. Then, all at once, the wolfhound turned his head. He had sensed their presence and with tremendous strength, leapt through the waves and rushed, barking deafeningly, towards the intruders. The three dogs fled, terrified, back the way they had come and the seal also vanished underwater, startled by the rumpus. Jack and Zoe managed to reach the tunnel and run up it, fear lending them additional speed, but Bertram was too slow and the wolfhound was upon him before he had reached the rear of the cave.

'You!' cried the giant. 'Why are you here?' He had calmed down somewhat on recognizing the old boxer.

'I – I – didn't mean any harm,' Bertram stammered. 'Just – just inquisitiveness, you see.'

'Yes,' said Liam. 'I have discovered that about you already.' He looked closely at Bertram as if examining him. 'Did you see my master's relics?'

'Relics? I – no,' answered the boxer uncertainly.

'Oh, very well then.'

Bertram was racking his brains. Relics? All at once he realized. 'You mean the, er, pieces of clothing?'

The wolfhound looked angry. 'You did see them then!'

'Yes, but I didn't understand. . . . I thought nothing of them.'

'Ah well,' said Liam in a softer tone. 'Why shouldn't I tell you? You're no threat to me. They're precious to me, you see, because they're from my master. From time to time things – those things – would come ashore on the tide. I used to find them here. I collected them for – well, his return, and I guard them for him.'

Bertram looked at him sadly. What faithfulness! 'Your master . . . must, I think . . . have been very proud of you.'

Liam didn't answer. He looked out seaward. 'Seal's gone,' he muttered. 'You've made me go hungry.'

'You eat – seals?' Bertram whispered in amazement.

'Of course I don't eat seals!' boomed the wolfhound. 'What a ridiculous idea. How could I catch one, even if I wanted to?'

'I'm sorry, I just don't understand.'

'Of course you don't. Why should you? Well – Seal and I eat together.'

Jack and Zoe had crept back down the passage, having heard the calmer, almost friendly voice answering Bertram's. Despite their initial fright they were also very curious to learn more, and peeked round the corner of the tunnel, unbeknownst to the wolfhound. Bertram guessed they were there, but he didn't let on because he thought Liam would be readier to explain to an audience of one.

'What do you and, er, Seal eat?' he enquired.

'Fish, naturally. What else would a seal feed on?'

'I don't know,' Bertram answered. 'Until tonight I'd never seen such a creature.'

'I see.' The wolfhound looked around, as if reminded of something. 'You weren't alone in my bay, I think?' he asked. At once Jack and Zoe retreated a few paces.

'I wasn't,' Bertram admitted. 'I have two friends on the island, but you've no cause for alarm. They're harmless and only came with me at my insistence. As you see, you soon frightened them off.'

'Oh, I don't mean to terrorize anyone,' Liam said. 'I'm a little jealous of my master's things and I reacted too strongly. I prefer solitude; no doubt you have sensed that. But I don't object to your presence – it's not my island. I don't want to be here and I shall leave as soon as my master reclaims me.'

Bertram changed the subject quickly. He wanted to learn more about the wolfhound's eating habits before he became too sad.

'How do you hunt the fish?' he asked.

'Seal finds them'

'He *catches* them for you?' Bertram couldn't believe it.

'No, he doesn't catch them. *I* catch them,' was the answer. Bertram was even more puzzled.

'It's a partnership,' said Liam by way of explanation, 'a partnership born out of the same misfortune. Seal suffered in that storm just as I did. Like many of his kind he used to follow fishing boats to feed from titbits or fish that escaped from the humans' nets. Well, he was circling our boat when the storm suddenly blew up. Seal was caught up on a huge swell and flung against the side of our boat, with such violence that he was badly hurt. Despite his terrible injuries, he still managed to help me ashore, buoying me up when I threatened to sink by swimming underneath me. He knew me and my boat from old and so he helped me rather than let me drown. Now I help him. He can no longer bite, but he rounds up the shoals of fish and drives them ashore. I snap them up where I can in shallow water, usually with some success. Anyway, whatever I catch and kill I bring ashore, and bite into chunks. Then Seal swims in and we share the catch. He swallows his at a gulp.'

'What a marvellous way of working together,' Bertram commented. 'It's the most wonderful thing I ever heard. And the seal knows you are waiting for your master here?'

'Of course. He knows as much about the storm and its consequences as I do. We understand each other.'

'Do you – communicate?'

'We make our own noises and, after all this time, we have a good idea of each other's intentions. Of course the partnership happened naturally. Seal was starving and – well, I was brought up on fish, my master being a fisherman. We both seemed instinctively to know what the other needed. The method of our fishing was developed over a long period; at first we made lots of mistakes but now we survive easily.'

'I'm so very sorry we drove Seal away,' Bertram apologized. 'I see now just what damage was done by our curiosity.'

'He'll be back,' Liam said shortly. 'Tomorrow night he'll be here again.' He looked Bertram over penetratingly. 'You've heard my story now, all of it. How did *you* get here? You're not an island dog.'

Bertram suddenly felt extremely awkward. By comparison with the wolfhound's battle for survival, their escapade seemed rather frivolous. He didn't know how to answer.

'Are you lost?' Liam prompted.

'Er, no, not lost. One of my companions lives on this island and the other one – and myself – came over here on his master's boat to, um, keep him company,' the boxer finished lamely.

'Keep him company? What do you mean? If he has his master, this other dog, why does he need your company? And where is *your* owner?'

Bertram was silent; there was just nothing he could say

to that. But he was thinking deeply.

'I won't disturb you any longer,' he said at length. 'I apologize again and I hope Seal will put in another appearance tonight.'

'Too late now,' said Liam. 'The fish will have scattered. And you – where do you eat?'

'We're fed by the Good People.'

'I don't know what you mean,' the wolfhound returned, 'but we'll let it rest. There's only one Good Person as far as I'm concerned; I care absolutely nothing for any others.'

Bertram began to walk back through the cave to the tunnel.

'We may see each other again,' Liam boomed after him. 'You know where to find me if you choose.'

Bertram paused, surprised by the giant's veiled invitation, but didn't reply as he continued on to the passage.

'Foolish animals,' the wolfhound murmured to himself. 'They've put themselves in a trap.'

10

Recognition

When Jack and Zoe saw Bertram was leaving safely, they lost no time in scampering back along the rock passage to the cliff top, and both were thankful to be once more in the open air. Here they waited, listening to Bertram's laboured progress along the tunnel. The old boxer was badly out of breath when he at last emerged and it was a while before he could talk. His head hung down as he gasped and wheezed after his efforts.

'We heard your discussion,' Jack told him. 'That's a peculiar set-up: a seal and a dog. And what would happen to the giant, I wonder, if anything became of the seal?'

'Don't talk like that,' Zoe begged. She had immediately imagined a ravenous wolfhound, desperate for some other source of food.

Bertram understood her reaction. 'I told you – before,' he panted. 'He's no threat – to us. But hasn't – another – thought occurred to you?'

'Another thought? No, what do you mean?'

'You saw the way he treasures those pathetic relics of his master.' Bertram reminded her. 'Doesn't that make our presence here an awful irony, when we have the benefit of masters and mistresses to feed and shelter us and yet we've turned our back on them?'

Zoe gaped. 'I hadn't actually—' she began.

'You decided to come here,' Jack broke in resentfully, addressing himself to the boxer. 'I didn't get the idea you thought you were very well cared for, but already you're having second thoughts!'

'Yes, now it's too late,' Bertram answered. 'In my case it was the prospect of a spell in the kennels that I hate which persuaded me. But Zoe here had only a vague idea of some sort of adventure which drew her to the island. Just to relieve the boredom of winter!'

'Don't, Bertram,' Zoe pleaded in alarm. 'Don't make it sound as if we made a mistake. It's all that great dog's fault. Why did you have to go and talk to him? He's nothing to us.'

'You forget, Zoe,' Bertram reminded her drily, 'it was Jack's tales of the giant and such like which aroused your interest in the first place. I knew nothing about him.'

Jack was becoming impatient. He didn't like the way Bertram had begun to push himself forward. It was *his* island, but for a while now he had felt that Bertram, a stranger, was trying to be the leader of their little group. Also, he was putting doubts in Zoe's mind about her being there at all when he, Jack, had only invited the old dog to persuade Zoe to make the trip in the first place. Bertram was certainly beginning to sour the arrangement. 'Look, Bertram,' he said, trying to sound reasonable, 'why spoil things? Forget the wretched Liam and let's—'

'Yes, you would say that,' broke in Bertram. 'Forget him – poor animal – when you have your master and home all secure at the back of you. Don't you have any sympathy?'

'Not much,' Jack admitted, and now even Zoe looked at him sharply, astonished.' The dog's obviously out of his mind, sitting up there day after day to no purpose. If his master was alive he'd have come by now, wouldn't he? Yet *he* can't accept it.'

Bertram and Zoe were both taken aback at Jack's apparent callousness. Then the boxer said quietly, 'Perhaps he daren't accept it.'

There was an awkward silence. The mongrel realized he had gone too far and regretted it. He wasn't cruel, only inclined to be selfish. 'I didn't mean to sound brutal,' he muttered. 'Only we can't help him, can we? We can't bring his master back. There's nothing we. . . .' His voice tailed off. 'I'm sorry,' he added.

Zoe yawned. She felt disappointed in Jack, but didn't want to think too deeply about his motives. Now she said, 'Let's forget it. I'm tired and you must be too, Bertram. Let's go to our sleeping place. Jack, you'll be going home, I think?'

'I am, straight away.' He seemed almost glad to be leaving them.

They trotted together back through the wood and then Jack bade them farewell and went his own way. Bertram and Zoe nestled into their little den and, pressing against each other, tried to sleep. Neither could. Bertram had put doubts in Zoe's mind and, as for the old boxer himself, he was trying to think of a way in which he could get Jack on his own. He wanted to ask the mongrel what possibility there was of getting off the island if he or, more particularly Zoe, wanted to go home. The wolf-hound's predicament had made him realize just how vulnerable he and Zoe were, though in a different way. Of course the last thing Bertram wanted to do was raise the topic in front of the little terrier. He knew she would begin to fret, if she hadn't done so already, and Jack might not prove to be helpful.

In the darkness, the image of the great dog standing shoulder deep in the sea, and beyond him the seal, flitted across Bertram's mind. It seemed such an unlikely arrangement, yet it worked perfectly and had done so for a long time, without anyone finding out. Bertram's thoughts then turned to the master and mistress he had deserted. For that was the word for his flight: it *was* desertion and he felt guilty, though he doubted if he would ever have acknowledged this to himself before his conversation in the cave with Liam. He guessed Zoe was almost certainly experiencing the same feelings of remorse.

They slept fitfully and at dawn Bertram was awake, shivering slightly in the October chill. He waited, as the light grew, for Zoe to stir. When the terrier awoke she stretched elaborately, looked at Bertram and said, 'Food.'

'Yes,' said the boxer. 'Just what I was thinking.'

No further mention was made by either of the wolfhound or anything to do with him. They set off for the monastery, arriving much too early, and waited patiently for an age for the Good Person to make his appearance. The cats wandered in through the archway at odd intervals. Despite the regular amounts of food these animals ate they never seemed to put on any weight, and Zoe remarked on it.

'Perhaps we shall end up looking as scrawny as they are if we stay here, living rough and eating scraps,' Bertram said, looking fixedly at her. Zoe looked away quickly – she didn't want to think about that.

Jack arrived on the scene promptly as the food was being brought out: his instinct was faultless. Bertram realized there might be an opportunity here to talk to him, if he could finish eating before Zoe, which he usually did since he was far less delicate. This day he wolfed his portion down almost without tasting it, then he lumbered across to the mongrel who was sitting in his customary position in the middle of the courtyard.

'You looked famished,' Jack remarked.

Bertram grunted. 'Never mind about that,' he said. 'I

want to ask you something. If Zoe and I wanted to leave the island, how would we do so?'

Jack looked suspicious. 'What are you saying? Zoe has never said so much to me.'

'No, no. I said *if* we wanted to – you know, at some time later on. Could we hide on your master's boat again?'

'You could, but it wouldn't do you any good,' Jack answered unhelpfully.

'Why not?'

'I told you: when the season ends we come back here for the winter. He doesn't make any crossings at all until the spring comes.'

'But – but – what will we do until then?'

'Stay here with me.'

Bertram lost his temper. 'We *don't* stay with you, do we?' he snapped. 'You're in your cosy home with your master's food; we're living out in the open. What if the Good People run out of food?'

'Don't be silly, Bertram. Even you must know humans never run out of food. My master fetches food from the village when we need some. And just because it's winter doesn't mean supplies don't reach the island from the mainland.'

'Ah!' Bertram seized on this. 'A boat brings them, does it?'

'Of course.'

'How often?'

'How should I know? That's the concern of humans. But I have occasionally seen these boats – they're big and slow and tall, nothing like the one my master and I own.'

'So there is a way out – I mean if we have to go back,' Bertram insisted.

'I suppose so,' Jack allowed. 'But I don't know when. Those boats come here very rarely, I should think; I haven't seen them more than once or twice.'

'We'll leave it now,' said Bertram. 'I don't want to worry Zoe.' He had noticed she had finished and was coming over.

Jack thought it likely that Bertram had already put the idea of leaving in Zoe's mind, and decided that he must make her forget all about it. He knew she admired him and greatly enjoyed his company; now he set out to make her like him even more, and if possible, get her away from Bertram.

'What have you two been talking about?' Zoe asked innocently.

Both dogs looked guilty, as if their secret thoughts showed on their faces. 'I'll go and drink,' Bertram said hurriedly and waddled off to the water-bowls.

'You two are up to something,' Zoe said.

'No, nothing,' Jack assured her. 'I was only thinking how marvellously lucky I am to have such a friend as you.'

Zoe's eyes lit up. Jack leapt high in the air and barked joyfully. Then he pranced around her playfully, trying to jump over her little body, first one way, then the other. The cats took fright and fled. They loathed the sound of barking and could only keep their heads if the dogs were quiet.

'Come on, Zoe. Let's chase them!' cried Jack. 'Bet we could catch one.' He raced out of the courtyard, saw one of the cats pelting towards the village and was after it in a flash. Zoe followed his lead and Bertram was left watching them blankly, his jowls dripping water.

The cat ran fast. It had no time to look for a tree and there was nothing else to climb. Jack's flying bounds brought him closer, while Zoe's little legs meant she fell behind. The cat got through a garden gate, wove in and out of plants and finally scrambled up a forsythia shrub.

It was a young bush and the cat swayed and dipped dangerously on the slender branches. The animal was no more than a metre from the ground, and with its every movement, threatened to bring the shrub down. Jack vaulted the gate athletically and, yapping excitedly, jumped up and down underneath the plant, each jump almost bringing him level with the terrified fugitive. Zoe, meanwhile, paused at the gate, unable to get over. She whined in exasperation, unable to see what Jack was up to, and scratched in vain at the obstacle in her path.

Finally, the cat lost its footing and tumbled in an undignified heap, sprawling on the soil underneath where it spat furiously at Jack, arching its lean back in a vain attempt to appear larger than it was. Jack was in a frenzy, snapping this way and that at the cornered beast, while Zoe hurled herself at the gate in her efforts to see what was happening. Suddenly a human voice rang out.

'Jack! Come here! What on earth are you doing?' It was Seaman Halebury.

Zoe glanced up at the man who stood next to her, looking into the garden where his dog was making such a commotion. Seeming very ashamed of himself, the mongrel came at his master's bidding, leaping back over the gate and leaving the terrified cat to make its escape.

'Scatter!' Jack hissed to Zoe and she ran, though she needn't have worried. Unaccompanied by an elderly boxer, Jack's master wouldn't easily have identified her. He had no reason to suspect she was on the island and other people's dogs were not of much interest to him anyway.

Zoe automatically retraced her steps. She saw Bertram plodding towards her and, at the sight of him, the terrier all at once felt intensely irritated. How slow and unexciting the old dog could be, compared with the live wire Jack. Jack was the one who made things happen, who led her on adventures she'd never have had with boring old Bertram. And now Jack was with his master, and there was nothing to do and no possibility of any fun in his absence. She took one more look at the boxer's bandy legs, his stiff gait and his grizzled muzzle snorting for breath, and bolted. She ran through the tiny village, and on and on until her disappointment and her exasperation were eased a little. Then she slumped down where she was on the turf, panting and hot with exertion. How long would it be before Jack could return? His master might take him home for the rest of the day. What could she do on her own? Oh, it was insufferable. She even contemplated going up to the giant's vantage point, but she hadn't quite the courage to do that. She rolled over and twisted and turned, giving her back a good scratch. At last she had no choice but to go back to the sleeping quarters – what Bertram had begun to call their 'den' – so that Jack could find her easily if he managed to return.

Bertram, of course, had eventually got close enough to see Jack with his master. His first thought was to make himself scarce before Seaman Halebury saw him, but then he stopped. Things had changed. Perhaps it would be a good thing if the man were to recognize him. The question then would be: what would he do? Would he think Bertram's owners were on the island and that they'd lost him? At any rate, it was a good bet that if Bertram were to be identified as the old boxer from the Pier End Shop at Multon, Seaman Halebury would make efforts to reunite him with his master and mistress. That's the sort of thing humans did for each other, Bertram knew that. So he waited expectantly.

The seaman went into the village store and was inside for quite a time making his purchases, while Jack sat obediently outside. He dare not run after Zoe but he saw Bertram sitting, as he thought stupidly, in full view. 'Go away, Bertram!' he barked to him. 'You'll be seen. My master's inside.'

'I know,' the old dog replied coolly and came even closer.

'But – but – whatever are you up to?' Jack demanded. 'Oh, I see, you *want* him to see you. The game's over as far as you're concerned, is it? You want to give up?'

Bertram didn't answer directly. 'I'm interested in seeing what will happen,' he explained.

'Well, you'll soon discover that,' Jack said angrily. 'He's coming out.'

The man stepped from the shop, clutching his packages to him. He bade Jack follow him, scarcely glancing at the boxer. As they walked off together, Bertram followed. Jack kept looking round; he was furious and his eyes glittered with anger. 'Get away, you old fool!' he snapped. 'He doesn't want you!'

'Stop that yapping, Jack,' Halebury commanded his dog, but turned to see the cause of it. There was Bertram, obstinately plodding in the rear, only a metre or so behind. Again the seaman didn't seem to pay much attention to the other dog. He had no grounds for suspicion and had other things on his mind just then. Bertram began to fall behind, then suddenly, Halebury swung round and stared at the boxer for a long time. Rather put out by the steady human gaze, Bertram nevertheless saw a gleam of recognition in the man's eyes. He remembered the West Highland White he had seen recently and at last made the connection between Jack and his two beach playmates.

The man walked back and spoke to Bertram reassuringly. He wanted him sufficiently quiet so that he could look at the collar which the boxer, of course, was still wearing. Yes, there was the name of the owners, Locke, and their address. Now where were *they*? He ought to find them. And where had the West Highland White disappeared to? If he could find her he could probably find her owners too. Halebury pondered how these people had come to the island out of season – as far as he knew they had no craft of their own. He decided that for some reason they must have come over on the mail boat. This was a regular vessel which Jack had deliberately not told Bertram about.

Events were now in human hands. The dogs' plans or hopes had to be shelved for the moment, and despite Jack's fury he was powerless. Halebury walked back to the village store where he explained the situation to the shopkeeper, leaving Bertram and the packages in his care while he began to search for Bertram's owners. He didn't know Mrs Locke, but her husband, the owner of the pier-end shop, was a very familiar face. Jack was left to his own devices, and as soon as he saw Bertram was shut safely indoors, he concentrated on the need to alert Zoe. He didn't know where she had run to but, above all things, he didn't want his master to find her first. That would put a swift end to their companionship.

Luckily Jack chose to look in the likeliest place at the outset. Zoe greeted his arrival at the den with delight, but he soon quietened her with the news.

'Bertram? Taken?' Zoe was alarmed.

'Yes, and now my master's looking for you. You'll never escape him. He knows every inch of the island by heart. Only – wait! There is one place.'

'Where! Where?' Zoe cried. The idea of being hunted, even by a kindly dog-lover, frightened her.

'The giant's cave,' Jack announced.

'Oh no, no, how could I? Not on my own . . . ,' she began.

'I'll be with you,' said Jack. 'But quickly, there's no time to be lost. If we can get through the wood before anyone sees us, we're safe.'

'But what about Bertram? We can't just abandon him,' wailed the terrier.

'There's nothing we can do for him. He'll have to do the best he can,' Jack answered. He was secretly hoping the boxer was out of the picture for good, so tiresome had he become recently. 'Come *on*, Zoe, it's no good hovering there like that!'

She obeyed him and they ran helter-skelter for the wood, not pausing until they passed the solitary rowan tree which marked its far boundary.

Liam was sitting at his post, gazing out to sea. The two small dogs crept warily up to the tunnel entrance. In the daylight it was easy to find, and they stole quietly into the passage without disturbing the watcher.

'Can't – can't we just stay here out of sight?' Zoe said quietly. 'You know the giant doesn't like others going into his cave because of the – the – mementoes he keeps.'

'Perhaps you're right,' Jack replied, 'though I don't think he'd know. We could hide until just before dark and then creep out again. My master will've given up by then.'

'Yes, but poor Bertram,' Zoe whined. 'Where will he be?'

'I don't know,' said Jack, and there was a hard edge to his voice Zoe had heard only once before. 'I think,' the mongrel continued, 'you'll have to accept that you may have seen the last of that silly dog for quite some time.'

11

Separated

Seaman Halebury walked smartly towards Clany harbour. It wasn't the day for the mail packet but he wanted to make absolutely sure the boat hadn't crossed over, instead of on the usual Wednesday, because of a bad weather forecast. He very soon discovered there were no craft whatsoever on which the dogs' owners could have crossed from the mainland. So could they have come some days ago? And were they now staying for a spell with friends? That seemed unlikely unless the two couples knew the same people. Halebury, of course, knew everyone on Clany and wasn't aware of any visitors staying anywhere. In October the island was very quiet and he felt sure he would have known, but maybe some news had bypassed his isolated cottage. He returned to the village store.

'Don't suppose you know of any visitors staying in the village?' he asked the storekeeper.

'Not that I know of, Eddie,' was the reply.

'I thought as much.'

'Why?'

'Well, this dog sitting in your shop so quietly,' and Halebury indicated Bertram who looked at him expectantly, 'belongs in Multon, by the pier actually. How did he get here without his owners?'

'Couldn't have. They must be here somewhere,' the storekeeper said with conviction.

'But there's another one, too, Peter,' the seaman went on. 'Another dog, I mean. A little white terrier, who don't belong hereabouts either. I've seen this old chap and the terrier countless times together on Multon beach – they come and romp around with my Jack. And now they're both over here. What d'you make of it?'

'I don't know, I'm sure,' was the reply. 'Were the owners over here recently and the dogs got lost?'

'That's what I'm wondering,' said Halebury. 'I'm going to do some asking round. If no one knows anything I'll have to arrange for the dogs to go back, won't I? I'll take the old boxer off you now. He can come home with me for a bit. But I don't know where the other one's gone to. If you see a West Highland White running about, see if you can catch her, will you?'

'Certainly I will,' said the shopkeeper. 'Let me know how you get on.'

The seaman took a piece of string from the pocket of his anorak, secured it to Bertram's collar, retrieved his purchases, and led Bertram out of the shop. The boxer followed him without objection.

It didn't take Halebury long to make the rounds of the village but no one knew anything about the dogs or how they had come to the island. On his way home the seaman called in at the farm where Jack had taken Zoe to see his playmate, the little girl. The girl's mother said she had seen both the dogs the previous day with Jack, but she knew no more than that and had been puzzled about them herself. Halebury went on home, Bertram continuing to allow himself to be led.

Having shut the boxer in, Halebury decided finally to go down to the harbour and see if any of the fishermen who anchored their boats there could give him any information. He hoped to find the terrier on his way and try to catch her too. He had a shrewd idea that his own dog might lead him to her; Jack was permitted to run all over the island but Halebury knew he would return before dark – maybe with the terrier in tow.

At the harbour Halebury drew a complete blank. He was now pretty certain the two stray dogs had somehow got themselves to the island on a boat without their owners' knowledge. He felt the most likely explanation was that they had been playing around on the other side of the water, had fallen asleep in a boat and woken up to find themselves transported to the island. But which boat? And who was the skipper who had unwittingly shipped the live cargo?

In Seaman Halebury's cottage Bertram lay down placidly to wait for him to return with Zoe. He was convinced she would easily be found, but he hadn't reckoned on Jack's influence.

Jack and Zoe were very uncomfortable in the tunnel. The rock floor was cold and hard and rather than lie around, they kept running up and down, first to one end, then the other.

'Why don't we go down to the beach?' Jack suggested. 'It's so murky in here.'

'No, Jack, I'd be afraid of being noticed by the watcher up there,' Zoe replied, referring to Liam. 'He'd come after us, I'm sure, if he thought we were disturbing his treasure.'

'He looks out to sea,' Jack reminded her. 'He wouldn't see us.'

But Zoe wouldn't be persuaded and would only venture just inside the cave where they could, at least, see each other properly and watch the waves breaking over the sand.

'Oh, I do hope Bertram comes soon,' Zoe said worriedly. She always felt insecure when her old companion wasn't with her. Jack was lively and exciting but his presence failed to convey the same reassurance. And now he became irritable.

'How can he come, Zoe?' he snapped. 'That's just what we don't want him to do!'

'Why not?'

'Because he wouldn't be on his own, would he? I told you!'

'Perhaps he'll escape.'

'Nonsense. My master will see that he doesn't. What's so special about an ancient boxer, anyway, who can hardly put one leg before the other? *I'm* here, aren't I?'

'You didn't use to speak like that about him,' Zoe said accusingly, ignoring the last remark. 'I thought you liked him.'

'Yes, well, that was— Oh! He just gets on my nerves,' Jack replied. 'He wants everything done the way he likes it – slowly.'

'He can't help being old,' Zoe said. She was surprised to find herself defending Bertram so stoutly, and moreover actually feeling hurt on his behalf by Jack's carping.

'I wish he'd never come here. He'd have been better off in his kennels,' Jack said savagely. 'We'd have been having a much more adventurous time; everything would have been more lively. And now he's ruining all our plans.'

'But you persuaded him to come!' Zoe was astonished.

'No, *you* persuaded him,' said Jack. 'I only suggested he came because I knew you wouldn't have come without him.'

Zoe felt miserable and very alone. She seemed to be discovering a different Jack from the one she thought she knew. 'Don't let's argue,' Jack said more reasonably. 'We must stay friends at all costs.'

'Yes,' Zoe answered quietly. But she was still unhappy.

Later Jack tried to get her to play a game with him, chasing around the back of the cave and up and down the tunnel, but Zoe could only join in half-heartedly. She was listless and eventually just lay down, put her head on her paws and sighed. The approach of dusk took forever.

Jack disturbed her dreams. 'I think we could risk moving,' he said. 'It's getting darker and it's raining. My master won't be searching for you now, I'm certain.'

They ran back along the passage and out into teeming rain. Before they had gone more than a few quick paces, they ran headlong into Liam who, head down, was making for his cave.

They stood stock still, and Liam stared at them for what seemed an eternity.

'I know who you are,' he said at last. 'What are you doing here, and where's Bertram?'

'We – we're hiding,' stammered Jack, shrinking back towards the passage. 'Bertram's somewhere else,' he ended lamely. Zoe was surprised to see him cringing like that in front of the wolfhound.

'Have you been in my cave?'

'No. No, no,' Zoe answered at once. 'Not the cave – only, you know, the tunnel. . . .'

'Oh. And why was that?'

'Sheltering,' Jack said quickly.

'Then why have you left it now?'

'We have to go home.'

'*Home?*'

'Yes, well, to Bertram,' Jack lied.

Liam wasn't convinced. 'What exactly are you up to?' he enquired coolly.

'Zoe here is hiding from my master, and I followed her into the tunnel,' said Jack. 'He wants to take her off the island.'

'Oh, now I see. But why should he want to do such a thing? Don't you have a master of your own, Zoe?'

'Yes, and a mistress,' she replied innocently. 'But they're not here.'

Liam stared at her incredulously. 'Then why ever are you on the island?' he boomed. 'It doesn't make sense.'

'We must go, it's very wet,' said Jack, making a dash past the wolfhound and leaving Zoe to fend for herself.

Liam bent to the terrier who showed signs of dithering. 'If you need a dry spot later, I don't mind if you come my way,' he offered kindly. 'This is weather for seals, not dogs.' Then he was gone.

Jack came bounding back. He shook his coat hard and said to Zoe, 'I must go on. Once my master sees me return you'll be safe.'

'You're not going to *leave* me?' she asked, her voice tremulous.

'Well, yes. My master will be suspicious if I don't turn up, won't he? It's only for tonight, Zoe.'

'The whole night? But, but I've never been on my own in a strange place before. Where can I go? Oh, Jack!'

'Don't worry, it's quite safe. You'll go to your den, of course.'

'But I shall be soaked.'

'Get under cover.'

'The plants will be soaked, too, and they'll drip all over me. Do I have to suffer that all night?'

'How about the caves then? I told you about the one that always stays dry,' Jack said. 'Bertram didn't think a lot of it, but it's worth remembering in weather like this. *Do* you remember it?'

'Of course I do,' Zoe answered crossly. 'But I may not use *that* cave.'

Jack didn't appreciate the significance of this remark, though he was to think of it later. 'I'll run on home now,' he said. 'I'll come and find you in the morning as soon as I can and we'll have plenty of fun together.'

Zoe watched his black and white body race ahead through the pelting raindrops. She realized he didn't care at all about leaving her to struggle on by herself to find shelter, wherever that was. She had mistaken him; he was a fair weather companion indeed. She missed Bertram terribly.

The rain continued to drive down. Only in the wood was there some protection for her, but very little even there. Her long coat was plastered along her back and against her sides; mud splashed its whiteness and gave her a bedraggled, uncared-for appearance. Zoe knew nothing of that and, if she had, she wouldn't have cared. She longed for warmth and a dry basket – they were all she could think about. The den was as unwelcoming as she had expected. Not only was it devoid of friendly company, but the bracken was beaten flat, and the gorse and broom cascaded with water-drops. Zoe went on down to the beach, carefully stepping between or around rocks and boulders. Now she found that she didn't remember at all which was the dry cave. She entered two, both of which were horribly cold, damp and forbidding in the deep blackness. She became more and more frightened. At last in the third cave she found a dry spot, but couldn't settle. The noise of the sea and the rain falling outside were such lonely, eerie sounds, they heightened her sense of solitude. She started to imagine strange things – creatures of the night on their nocturnal prowls, human voices calling her from across the sea, the body of Liam's fisherman washed ashore. Leaping up, her whole body quaking, she raced from the cave on to the black, mysterious beach, but didn't stop. She ran back to the den but didn't stop there either; she just kept running, on to the wood, and through it. Suddenly she realized where she was running. She was running towards the promise of company – any company that might be offered on such a comfortless and fearsome night. She found herself back in the rock passage where she had passed the daylight hours. At the end of the passage Zoe paused, listened and sniffed the cave entrance. The salty, musty odour of the place was unchanged. In the gloom she couldn't tell if the wolfhound was there or not.

'Are – are you there?' she called hesitantly.

There was no answer and her anxious voice could scarcely have been heard anyway above the thrashing of the sea, which was being whipped up by the beginnings of a storm. She padded over the pebbly floor to the cave entrance. For a while she could make out nothing. The moon and stars were completely obscured by black storm clouds and the beach, too, was a mass of featureless grey. If Liam was on the beach, she couldn't see him.

The wind, strengthening rapidly, blew Zoe's fur dry as she stood vainly searching the foreground with her black button eyes. Then the rain returned in a savage squall, dashing itself against her and soaking her all over again. Zoe retreated a few steps inside the cave mouth, but not before she had noticed movement farther along the beach. It was difficult for her to make out what had moved; there was just a shapeless blur of dim grey against the darker grey behind it. She guessed it must be Liam, for what other creature came to this spot? But she couldn't be sure, and her uncertainty made her tread farther back into the deep obscurity of the wolfhound's den.

She recalled the seal – perhaps that was what she had

seen? But no, she thought it couldn't have been. The movement had been on the beach, and Zoe mistakenly believed that seals never left the sea to come on dry land. Perhaps Liam was feeding. As she pondered she heard, through the rage of the storm, a tearing sound, terrifyingly loud. It seemed to come from above and all around her and she raced out of the cave in panic. Now she saw Liam galloping towards her, his huge legs taking gigantic bounds. A long way behind him another creature was hurrying, ungainly and painfully slow, over the sand, its belly hugging the ground as if it had lost all use of its limbs.

Liam saw the terrier and in his booming voice cried out, 'Get back inside! Hurry! The cliff is falling!'

There was a tremendous crash followed by a thud that was so massive it seemed to make the entire island reverberate. Zoe found herself bowled over and over, as the great dog hurled himself into the cave, knocking her small body flying. She struggled to her feet, gasping for breath. Liam made no apology in the stress of the moment for injuring her. Zoe only heard him murmur, 'Seal! Poor Seal! You shouldn't have come ashore.'

12

The Havoc of the Storm

Bertram was disappointed, but not unduly alarmed, when Seaman Halebury returned home alone. He guessed Jack and Zoe were together somewhere, and that Jack would soon lead her back. However, when the mongrel arrived at the cottage on his own, the old boxer was extremely worried. He tried to question Jack but, in front of his master, Jack didn't pay much attention to him.

There was a happy welcome on both sides when the mongrel arrived. Halebury gave him a rub and a pat, talking kindly to his pet; Jack's tail wagged boisterously and he licked the man's hands with great affection. Bertram was reminded again of the relationship with *his* master that he had turned his back on by coming to the island. Mr Locke was not unkind and occasionally showed his old dog great warmth. It was the mistress who made Bertram unhappy.

Halebury bustled about, preparing food for the two dogs. Bertram wasn't at all against a second meal, but he did think with a pang of Zoe who wasn't able to share it. Where was she? How could Jack have deserted her? As soon as they had eaten, Halebury left them to eat his own solitary meal of bread and cheese in the cottage's little dining room. Bertram wasted no time in pouncing on Jack.

'Where is she? Where's Zoe?' he demanded.

'In your den, of course,' Jack answered coolly.

'In this rain? On her own? How could you?'

'How could I what?'

'How could you leave her?' Bertram said angrily.

'I had to, didn't I? If I'd stayed, my master would have come after us.'

'Zoe's not used to being on her own and sleeping rough,' Bertram went on. 'With me shut up, you should've stayed with her. Why didn't you bring her here?'

'She didn't want to come here, of course,' Jack snapped back. 'It would have meant the end of her stay on the island. Why would she want that?'

'Oh, she doesn't know what she wants,' Bertram answered. 'She came here on an impulse. You made it sound exciting, but she didn't understand what was involved any more than I did. I do now, though, and I know we made a mistake. We're not cut out for sleeping on hillsides and in caves, begging for food with a lot of skinny cats!'

'Well, you certainly change your ideas quickly,' said Jack. 'You've only been here a day or so.'

'It seems like an age to me.'

'So you conveniently arranged for yourself to be collected and sheltered by the only human on the island who knows where you came from!'

'How was I to know Zoe would listen to you and hide herself away?'

'What did you expect her to do, Bertram? You gave up too easily. She's got more mettle.'

'You don't know anything about it,' the boxer retorted. 'I'm sure she's very happy lying outside on her own with the rain pouring down on her! Yes – and while you lie here in comfort, dry and warm.'

Jack did appear for a moment to feel sorry but he said quickly, 'If she's got any sense, she'll go into the cave I showed you. It's only till daylight anyway. Then I'll join her again.'

'What about me?'

'Well, you've booked your passage, haven't you? You'll be sent home.'

'I won't leave here without Zoe,' Bertram declared emphatically.

'You won't have any choice in the matter. My master knows your owner. D'you think he'll allow you to stay here now?'

Bertram was horrified. The idea of being carried back to the mainland whilst Zoe was left behind had never entered his head. 'But – but – Jack,' he spluttered, 'surely your master will wait until he's rounded up Zoe too?'

'Zoe's in hiding,' Jack reminded him coldly. Then, in a brighter tone, he added, 'We shall have lots of fun, the two of us, when you're gone.'

Bertram was aghast. 'You planned this,' he said quietly.

'Of course I didn't plan it!' Jack barked. 'You decided to have yourself recognized, not me. I warned you about that, didn't I?'

Bertram's head sank on his paws in misery. Suddenly he looked up and around, pulled himself to his feet and began to sniff all round the walls of the kitchen. Then he sniffed under the door.

'There's no escape,' Jack commented. 'My master will make sure you don't get out. He has a duty now, hasn't he?'

Bertram sank down again, utterly deflated. Outside, the wind howled and the rain jetted horizontally against the windows in short bursts. 'You *must* bring Zoe here then,' said the boxer.

'And if I don't?' Jack queried.

'If you don't, then you will prove that you really care nothing for her,' Bertram told him. 'Which is what I've suspected all along.'

'Of course I care,' Jack said resentfully. 'I love her company. She's perky and light-hearted and funny when she gets excited. Why should I want anything to—'

The mongrel's voice was drowned by a muffled but mighty thump that made the cottage windows rattle. Jack and Bertram barked together and their hackles rose; they sensed something awful had happened. Jack leapt on to a windowsill, straining to look outside into the darkness. His master came running in, grabbed his coat, pulled on his boots and, taking care the dogs didn't follow, hastily unlocked the door, forcing his way out into the teeth of the storm. The kitchen door slammed shut behind him. Halebury switched on his torch and made a quick tour of the garden and surrounding area, but could see nothing here that seemed out of order. The wind whistled and squalls of rain sent him hurrying back indoors. It was so black a night that it was useless to contemplate searching any further until morning.

He found Bertram and Jack cowering together in the kitchen, both frightened now by a sense of dread that filled the air. Bertram was sure that harm had come to Zoe; he didn't know how. Jack feared his neglect of her that night had placed her in danger it was now too late to avoid.

It was a long time before either Liam or Zoe dared to creep to the cave mouth to see what damage had been done outside. But, miraculously, when they did do so they found the seal lying in the entrance, apparently unharmed except for a deep cut on his back which had been caused by a falling rock.

'Seal! Seal!' Liam cried joyously. The great dog frisked about the bewildered but delighted animal, who watched him with his dark liquid eyes. The seal gave a little 'honk' of pain.

'He's wounded,' boomed the wolfhound. 'Look, on his back.'

Zoe came cautiously. She soon realized from the seal's expression that the strange beast was harmless. His gash was bleeding freely and, instinctively, she licked at it, soothing the hurt. The seal was comforted. He sighed.

'You've helped him,' said his friend Liam. 'He's telling me so. What's your name, little dog?'

'Zoe. I know yours.'

'Do you indeed? Seal and I were feeding on shore,' the wolfhound went off at a tangent. 'I'd caught quite a lot of fish. Then suddenly we saw the cliffside cracking and tearing and – we ran. Seal *can't* run,' he corrected himself. 'But you should see him in the water; diving and swimming like any fish. The sea's his true home; he doesn't like land.'

Zoe said, 'What happened – outside, I mean? Is it safe now?'

'I think so. Yes, we should take a look.'

Leaving the seal to rest, Liam and Zoe left the cave. To their right, the direction from which Liam had run for his life, the beach was unrecognizable. It was piled with mounds of rock, soil and plants, which had been ripped from the cliffside by the elements. Even in the darkness they could see a gaping hole like a great wound cut in the island's side.

'What – what's happened?' Zoe asked in awe as the storm that was still raging around them drove them back once more to shelter.

'The hillside has collapsed,' the wolfhound answered her. Inside the cave he started to think over what had happened. 'You may have made a mistake coming to visit me tonight,' he summed up.

Zoe's stomach gave a lurch. 'Why? Are we in danger? I came for comfort.'

'Don't worry, the cave's quite safe,' Liam assured her. 'But,' he added grimly, 'it might be all we're left with now.'

'I don't understand,' said Zoe, and she really had no inkling of what he was suggesting.

The wolfhound ran to the back of the cave, having first made sure that his master's relics were undamaged. He sniffed hard at the tunnel entrance, then stepped into the passage. With great care he went along it, a paw at a time; the tunnel smelt different to him and he suspected the worst. At last he knew he was approaching the cliff opening and went even more carefully. The wind rushed in at him from the cliff-top entrance, whipping up his long coat, and then he was at the end, staring out into a void, a space. A great chunk of the promontory, on which he had sat to look out to sea, had been torn away by the force of the storm. Cliff-top, turf and path no longer existed, and the tunnel now opened out into thin air. All the clay and turf surrounding it had been ripped away, and there was now only a sheer rock face above and below, dropping straight down to the sea. Liam's cave, its contents and occupants were now completely cut off by the sea at the front and by a granite wall at the back.

Liam retraced his steps slowly. Zoe's fate briefly occupied his mind, but his thoughts turned to the lost master he could now no longer watch for. He remembered the pathetic collection of belongings he had fetched from the tide and lovingly safeguarded. The fury of the present storm reminded him forcibly of that other storm which had parted him, for so long now, from the man he worshipped. The seal looked at Liam as he came back and gave him a little greeting, as if he understood what was troubling him.

'How are you, Seal?' the wolfhound asked gently, with the realization that he – Liam – was only one of three animals affected by this new misfortune.

The seal's eyes shone up at him, as if to say, 'lucky'. They understood each other.

'What did you find?' Zoe asked nervously. She guessed something was amiss.

'We're isolated, marooned,' Liam told her bluntly. 'There's no route out of here any more. The passage ends in – nothing.'

'No! No! It can't be!' wailed Zoe. 'I *have* to leave here. The Good People feed me. How am I to reach them?'

'You can't, Zoe. I'm sorry. We're all cut off. Seal's all right, he can swim away, but we have to stay here.'

'But – but – I only came for shelter. And company,' the frightened terrier whined. 'What about Bertram? And Jack?'

'They're all right,' he assured her. 'Don't worry, little dog, we'll survive. Seal can still help us and you'll have to learn to eat fish.' Liam went and lay down by his treasure. He wanted to be quiet to think about his master and what he should do.

Zoe watched him helplessly, the misery of her position weighing down on her. She had felt lonely before but that had been as nothing. Why had she come to this unhappy island? A mistaken sense of adventure, an attractive companion, and a misunderstanding of her previous situation. She had thought she was discontented with her rather dull life, but now she realized she would do any-thing to get back to it – the routine, the unchanging days, the comfort. How stupid she had been! What did she know of the lives other, more wretched creatures had to endure? She and Bertram should have stayed where they were. Her realization had come too late, however; she was trapped. Her only companions were a bereaved wolfhound obsessed with watching and waiting for a master who never came and never would come and a strange marine creature on whose existence they both had to rely to stay alive.

13

Where's Zoe?

Later in the night the storm died down. In Seaman Halebury's cottage Bertram stayed wide awake, wondering about Zoe. At the first faint peep of light he woke Jack, who was sleeping on his side in the same room. 'Jack! Jack!' he barked.

'What – what is it?' The sleepy mongrel sat up and yawned.

'I think it's getting light. You must move.'

'Move? What do you mean?'

'Go and find Zoe. Bring her to safety.'

'I'll go just as soon as I can, don't worry,' Jack answered. 'But how I'm supposed to get out of the house before my master allows me to is another matter!'

'Of course, I wasn't thinking,' Bertram acknowledged. 'I'm so concerned about her, you know. When do you expect he will let you out? You must catch her at the Good People's.'

'My master rises early. He eats his own food; then he feeds me – *us*, now. He opens up and lets me out after that, usually; sometimes he goes with me. He may want to exercise both of us. Whatever happens, as soon as I can, I'll run off.'

Bertram was satisfied for the time being. But, as it grew lighter, he became agitated again. There was no sign and no sound of the human inhabitant of the cottage.

'It's no good getting impatient, Bertram,' said Jack. 'It

won't help.' He was trying to sleep, but the boxer kept disturbing him. At last they heard noises from the man's bedroom and, soon afterwards, he came into the kitchen. He greeted both dogs cheerily and stomped about, rattling utensils and opening packets. Sunlight slanted in through one window, for the storm had long since passed. Outside everything dripped water; deep puddles had formed in the garden and several clumps of plants had been battered flat. Halebury ate his breakfast stolidly, staring out at the scene. Then he filled two flat plates with dog food and watched the animals eat.

Bertram's appetite was unaffected by his new situation. He finished quickly and stood over Jack while the mongrel licked his own plate clean. Halebury got his out-door clothes on, seemingly preparing for a walk. Picking up the same piece of string he had used on the previous day, he tied it to Bertram's collar, made it fast, then opened the door. He had no wish to risk the boxer's running off. Jack was allowed to run free, while Bertram was led along the garden path and through the gate. He plodded along obediently, only irritated by Jack's refusal to leave them. However, as soon as Halebury was assured that the boxer was sufficiently refreshed, he turned on his heel and they headed back to the cottage.

As if at a signal, Jack bolted. He went first of all to Zoe and Bertram's old den. Their scent was fading fast, particularly since the ground had been scoured by the storm, so he knew Zoe hadn't spend the night hours there. He guessed that she had made for the dry cave he had shown her. Running hastily down to the beach, he vaulted the smaller rocks and, ignoring the other caves, picked up her scent inside the weatherproof one. It was fresh: she *had* been there. Jack was encouraged, reckoning she must have avoided the worst of the storm. Now he made his way directly to the monastery courtyard, aware that Zoe would be hungry.

It was still very early when he got there. Zoe was nowhere to be seen and Jack wondered what route she had taken. He hoped she would be able to find her way there without difficulty on her own. The mangy cats, also, hadn't yet put in an appearance. Jack waited around, wandering away a little from time to time to see if Zoe was coming and looking in every direction. Eventually the cats began to assemble, for feeding time was coming. Jack knew that if Zoe didn't show herself when the bowls were brought she would miss out, so he decided to sit in the courtyard himself, hoping the Good Person might think he needed the food. Then when Zoe did arrive she could have his bowl. It was worth a try, even though he knew he would be recognized by the Good People as not being a stray.

The robed figure emerged as the clock struck nine. He looked around at the waiting animals, noting Jack was on his own, and presently deposited the food bowls. There were less than before and Jack wasn't sure if he had been taken into consideration or not. Deciding to stake a claim before the cats commandeered all the bowls, he trotted over to one, stood guard over it and growled when one of the cats showed signs of wanting to claim it. The cat hesitated but wasn't entirely put off.

'You don't eat here,' it said to Jack in a harsh voice, licking its lips and looking with longing at the food bowl. 'This is meant for us.'

'You've more than enough,' Jack answered coolly, although he knew perfectly well that they hadn't.

The cat wasn't beaten yet. It looked Jack up and down, taking in his relative size and trying to estimate his strength. 'Why aren't you eating then?' the cat challenged.

'I don't want the food,' Jack replied, easily. 'But I know a creature who does, very badly.'

The cat was taken aback. 'You're guarding it for another? An animal who's not even here?'

'Yes' said Jack, sensing attack and tensing himself. 'And I wouldn't waste any more words on me, if I were you. Your companions over there will have eaten *your* share soon.'

Now the cat was torn between retreat, if only to ensure a mouthful or two of food, and holding his ground in the hope of winning even more. It lifted one front paw, unsure which way to move. Jack watched the cat carefully as reluctantly it began to back away. Jack relaxed a little. He looked around – still no sign of the little white-haired terrier.

'Go and eat,' he urged the cat. 'If my friend doesn't turn up I'll leave this food untasted. That's a promise.'

The cat considered his offer. It didn't trust the mongrel any more than any other dog but there was no point in risking a fight if there was a chance the food might be won without confrontation. It rejoined the other cats and snatched a hasty few gulps of what was left.

Jack continued to stand guard, and eventually the other cats went to the water bowls. The mongrel thought he couldn't wait much longer; he was very anxious to locate Zoe and make sure she was all right. The cat who had approached him hung back against one wall as the others left the yard. It eyed Jack and the food bowl greedily. Jack stared back. Each animal waited for the other to make the first move: the cat emerged victorious. Jack decided the priority now was to find Zoe. He left the food bowl without further ado and, as soon as he had passed through the archway, the starving cat made a dash for it.

Jack first looked all round for the familiar white coat of the West Highland terrier. Satisfied she wasn't on her way to the monastery, he set off for the little wood. There was a faint possibility that she might be somewhere near it. He thought of the giant and decided that, as a last resort, he would even approach the wolfhound at his lookout.

The wood yielded nothing and Jack went on up the narrow cliff path. He very soon discovered things were not as he had known them, for the terrain was now very different. The path wandered much closer to the cliff edge than he remembered, finally petering out into nothing. Jack realized what must have happened and peered over the lip of the rock edge. He gulped nervously and backed away, but forced himself onwards. After a few paces more he realized Liam's pinnacle was gone, hurled to the beach by the wind and storm. Had Liam been thrown over with it? Once more Jack crept to the cliff edge, dreading to see the crushed and mangled body of the wolfhound below, or even that of – no, no, he shook *that* thought away. He saw no body and gasped his relief. But what he did see was the exposed end of the cliff tunnel, now halfway down the rock face and impossible to reach either by clambering down the sheer rock or by a leap into space. *And supposing Zoe had been in that tunnel?* He shied away from the landslip, just as he shied away from such a terrifying notion. Fear for Zoe leant wings to his feet and he turned tail and raced for home, his paws drumming the turf.

Seaman Halebury was not around when Jack arrived, panting heavily, at the door. The dog yapped impatiently to be let in, then realized that his master was absent. Bertram's barks of enquiry from the interior of the cottage alarmed Jack more than he liked to admit. How was he to explain Zoe's disappearance to the old boxer? How *could* he explain when he himself had no idea where she might be? No, that wasn't true. He *did* have an idea, but he could hardly bear to think it, let alone repeat it. He sat shivering outside the kitchen door and maintained silence.

Halebury was having a last look round for Zoe before

taking Bertram to the boat. He had made up his mind to make the crossing to the mainland and return Bertram himself, and the sea was calm enough now after its recent fury. He knew Bertram's owner at the pier-end shop, and decided that, if he couldn't find Mr Locke straight away, he would ask after him at his near neighbours at the Seagull Café.

Zoe, of course, was still hidden and, after eating lunch with a friend, Halebury pressed on home. Jack followed him into the cottage. In the man's presence Bertram kept quiet as the stout string was once more attached to his collar. He wondered where he was being taken this time. Jack was allowed to accompany them and it soon became apparent to the mongrel, much to his consternation, that his master was heading for the harbour. He hung back, not wanting to be near Bertram when the boxer realized he was to be taken back over the water. Although he had wanted to see Bertram gone so that he could have Zoe all to himself, the fact that she was lost meant he would have no company at all now if Bertram left.

Halebury walked unhurriedly but purposefully to where he kept his little dinghy moored in a friend's boathouse, bundled Bertram in, then stepped in himself. Jack had vanished. For a while Bertram made no fuss, not at first realizing what was happening to him. He did look around for the mongrel, as did Jack's master, but he had wisely made himself scarce. Halebury wasn't bothered; he would be over and back in not much more than an hour and he knew Jack could look after himself very well.

When Halebury had rowed to the *Crest*, which was anchored at its winter resting-place in the harbour, he lifted Bertram up and climbed aboard. The dog was heavy and it was an awkward manoeuvre. If Bertram had chosen to struggle they would both have ended up in the water, but the boxer allowed himself to be carried and deposited on deck. Then the rowing boat was hauled up and lashed to the side. Bertram didn't recognize the *Crest*, for he was still in something of a daze at suddenly finding himself away from land. He had somehow imagined Jack and Zoe would be joining him, although whether the man would fetch them or whether they would arrive by some other means he really hadn't considered.

Abruptly the craft's engine sputtered into life. The anchor was weighed and the *Crest* turned slowly in a half spiral and then pointed herself towards the mainland. The motion startled Bertram into life. He ran along the deck to Halebury's little wheelhouse and then back again, becoming more and more alarmed as Clany harbour dropped behind them. The craft made a turn and Bertram saw the coastline swing past, slowly at first and then with gathering speed. He began to whine anxiously, not knowing what was in store for him. All at once Liam's beach and cave passed before his eyes as he scrambled on to one of the bench seats to see over the side. And there was the wolfhound, surrounded by the mounds of fallen rock and other debris, sitting quite still and looking towards the *Crest*. By his side a little white figure stood, unmistakably the shape of poor Zoe. Bertram picked them out immediately and barked frantically, clawing at the woodwork. He jumped down and ran to the pilot, barking and barking to divert him, but Halebury took no notice. He was looking straight ahead towards Multon, his destination.

Bertram was beside himself. He barked incessantly and his barks took on a desperate, eerie note. From the dwindling beach Zoe's yaps of recognition and Liam's booming response echoed back at him. Still Halebury pressed forward, the boat's engine purring evenly and noisily as, with each moment, Bertram was carried

farther and farther away from his trapped friend. He
knew nothing, of course, about the cliff fall. But he
sensed disaster and, as the vivid white of Zoe's coat dwin-
dled to a mere dot, something impelled him into action.
Instinct perhaps – he was certainly unthinking. But
almost before Bertram had realized what he was doing,
he had clambered over the stern of the boat and jumped
into the sea, his eyes still focussed on that white pin-point
on the beach. He was lucky to be washed away from the
Crest by a mild swell, otherwise he might have been
mangled by the spinning propellor. Then he began to
swim, blindly, doggedly, across the great expanse that
separated him from his old companion. Halebury
noticed nothing.

This was nothing like the short swim he and Zoe had
made from the boat at the start of their unfortunate
adventure. The boxer's feeble old legs soon began to lose
their strength and the beach seemed as far away as ever.
In the near distance, he saw a flat-topped lump of rock
just poking its head above the waves that washed, every
now and then, over its surface. He aimed for this with his
waning strength, knowing it was his only hope of avoid-
ing drowning. He struggled on, his paddling growing
weaker and weaker, his vision blurred. The rock
appeared to be no nearer. With a final kick or two in the
water, his limbs gave up the battle and gently, gradually,
he found himself sinking down, down, below the surface
of the sea and into ever darker and murkier depths.

14

Seal of Providence

By the time Bertram had jumped from the *Crest*, the boat was too far away for either Zoe or the wolfhound to see what had happened. All Zoe knew was that her only real friend on the island was gone and a feeling of desolation swept over her. She lay down, huddled against a rock, and her little body shook with misery. She was cold, ravenously hungry and very, very frightened. The thought of Jack didn't enter her head at all. She already felt that he had abandoned her and, in fact, the company of Liam was now more comforting to her. The great dog had promised her he would catch some fish as soon as his hunting partner should return, for, with the daylight, the seal had gone back to the sea. Zoe didn't relish the prospect of eating fish, though she knew she had no option. She lay with her head on her paws and wondered why Bertram was on the boat without her. Over and over again she tried to puzzle it out, but could find no solution. She could only guess that the man had taken him there, but why hadn't he rescued her too? How glad Bertram would be to get back home and be welcomed by his master and mistress. The thought of her own, in the Seagull Café, brought a fresh wave of misery that threatened to overwhelm her completely. Thankfully, Liam's deep voice diverted her.

'He'll come back for you,' he was saying, referring to the seaman. 'I'm sure he must have seen you.'

'I – hope – so,' Zoe forced herself to say, almost choking on the words that didn't want to come out. She wanted to be silent in her misery, yet she knew the wolfhound was trying to encourage her. And *he* had suffered too. How he had suffered! She tried to think about him and not be selfish.

'What will *you* do?' she whispered.

'Stay here, of course,' he answered at once. How tired he sounded. 'I have to wait. I couldn't leave until—' His booming voice left the rest unsaid, but he didn't need to finish. Zoe understood his plight only too well.

'You can't keep watch any more,' she said sadly.

'No. Not like I used to. But I – I'll watch from the beach for as long as I can.'

'And if his master comes,' Zoe murmured to herself, 'what would happen to Seal?'

Liam overheard and startled her by replying, 'I don't know. I've often wondered about that. We'll have to face that problem when it arrives. I wonder where Seal is now?' he added thoughtfully.

The seal wasn't very far distant; in fact he never swam a long way from Clany. His clumsy body was now transformed into a beautifully streamlined, sinuous suppleness, rippling through the cold, dark water towards the flurry of movement he had glimpsed as he rose to take in air. As he approached he took another look and saw the object in the sea begin to sink down and disappear underwater. He knew at once what was happening and hastened forward to give aid.

As Bertram sank down he had ceased to struggle. The cold water felt heavy and pressed on him remorselessly. Then suddenly he felt a nudge and all at once he was rising again, rather like a cork, to the surface. The waters broke over his head and he gasped and spluttered, gulping in great draughts of air. His poor old chest heaved and wheezed as he felt himself carried along, borne by something other than the current. This something buoyed him up from beneath, scarcely touching him, yet propelling him through the water. He watched the flat-topped rock he had set his sights on move nearer and nearer and then, abruptly, he was on top of it, cast up like a piece of sodden driftwood. He slithered to a halt over the slippery seaweed that clung to it and only just had time to glance around and see a dark shape skimming through the sea, its tail thrashing the water into foam as it dived out of sight. So Bertram stood on the rock, completely surrounded by a huge expanse of sea; an isolated and forlorn figure more dead than alive.

The *Crest* sped on minus its cargo. Halebury steered the boat into Multon, thinking happily about the joyful reunion he was soon to bring about. But when he turned to look for the dog, his heart skipped a beat. He thundered across the deck, then down into the tiny cabin, leaving the engine idling. Finding no sign of Bertram there, he raced back to the wheelhouse, turned his craft and headed once more towards Clany. Keeping one hand on the wheel, he grabbed his binoculars with the other and scanned the sea ahead, sweeping across the water's width from port to starboard. For a while he saw nothing; then at last he spied the flat-topped rock and its strange castaway. Halebury heaved a sigh of relief and brought the bows of the *Crest* in line. He dropped anchor some way off, not trusting his boat too close to the rock, which was well away from the usual crossing lanes between Multon and Clany. He had to lower the dinghy and row in to it.

Bertram was too exhausted to offer any resistance even

had he wanted to. He was very grateful for the man's appearance and surrendered his sopping body to Halebury's strong arms with a readiness which surprised himself. 'Dog overboard,' the sailor laughed to himself. 'Dog rescued.'

They were soon back on board. Halebury gave Bertram a brisk rub down with an old cloth and stowed him below in the cabin, where it was so warm the boxer promptly fell asleep.

The seal pulled himself up on to Liam's beach, calling to his friend to tell him what he had done. Zoe put her head on one side, listening to the unmusical honks with a baffled expression. Liam tensed. 'Something's happened,' he said, cocking his ears alertly.

'What?' cried Zoe, catching the other dog's mood.

'I think it's something urgent.' Liam left the terrier and padded down to meet the seal. 'You look pleased with yourself, Seal,' he said. And the seal did. His beautiful dark eyes shone excitedly and he honked again and again, turning to the sea and back repeatedly. Liam knew he had found something and wondered what it was. Then Seal came up close, looked Liam straight in the eye and gave his usual identifying honk, a soft one of recognition, which he always made as he approached the island to warn Liam to get ready for the fish he was bringing. The seal went on past the wolfhound, hauling himself laboriously over the beach until he reached Zoe. He gave her an identical greeting. Finally he turned and, looking out to sea in the exact direction of the flat-topped rock, gave the same sound for a third time. Liam understood the seal was deliberately linking the three friendly honks for some purpose and guessed the seal's message. They had known each other for a long time.

'Seal's seen your friend,' he called to Zoe.

'Bertram?' she asked hopefully.

'Yes, and I think there's more than that. He's very excited, making his swimming noises. Does Bertram swim?'

'Oh no, only if forced to. Oh, he must have fallen off the boat! Oh! Oh!'

'That's it!' Liam cried.

'He's drowned!'

'No, no, not drowned,' Liam assured her. 'Rescued. *That's* why seal looks so pleased. He rescued him, Zoe.'

The seal could see he was understood and gave two delighted honks of a more musical quality. He had quite forgotten about the wound on his back. Zoe noticed it still looked raw and red, put out her soft tongue and, as gently as before, licked it with a slow, soothing movement. The seal closed his eyes. He knew the dog's tongue could help him heal.

Liam shifted his gaze out to the empty sea, as he had done so many times before. 'Bertram must be back on land,' he said quietly. 'And you'll be the next to go.' His booming voice had a hollow, mournful ring to it; one of loneliness. Zoe paused in her task, but could offer no comfort. She followed up Liam's remark.

'And how would I go?' she asked.

'The same way as your friend the boxer.'

'But if it's not known where I am?'

'There could be another escape route for you,' the wolfhound said thoughtfully. 'There is a ship that comes into the harbour regularly bringing things for the island's humans. Oh, I've seen it countless times from my vantage point. It's always the same one – a red ship. Now, I'm almost certain that it goes back to your home area. If you could get on to that. . . .'

'If . . . if . . . ,' Zoe whined. 'How can I when we're completely cut off here? And oh, Liam, I'm so hungry.'

'There may be an answer,' said Liam. 'Let me think about it. And in the meantime—' He broke off and gave a special kind of bark to the seal. The animal looked at him for a moment and then began floundering back across the beach to the sea. Liam's bark had been a command.

'He understands the sound for food,' the wolfhound explained to Zoe. 'We must wait now on the shore.'

She followed him curiously and copied him as he stood motionless at the edge of the tide and stared intently ahead. For a long time nothing happened and she began to fidget. Her mouth ran with water and she swallowed hard over and over again. Liam didn't move a muscle; only his eyes occasionally blinked.

'Can you see anything?' he whispered suddenly.

Zoe stared at the waves until her eyes ached but she could make out nothing of interest. 'No,' she whispered back.

'Look, out there, beyond the darker water, where the sea glistens – don't you see the seal?'

Zoe saw nothing but she hated to appear stupid. 'Oh – oh yes,' she said.

'Now he'll come slowly in, pushing them before him. He swims up and down to prevent too many escaping.'

Zoe guessed that 'them' were the fish. At the thought of raw fish with its clean, tangy smell her jaws began to ache and her eager, open mouth dripped water. She was no fish-eater by habit but hunger overrode every instinct or preference. She put her head on one side, listening for the slightest sound of the seal's approach through the water. 'You won't hear him,' Liam said. 'He's entirely silent. Just follow him with your eyes.'

Zoe looked again and thought she saw a swirl amongst the banks of seaweed where the water looked dark. A sinuous shape powered its way just below the surface and, in front of it, darting silver flashes of sunlight on fish-scales showed where the seal's prey scurried here and there in their attempts to avoid him. She glanced at Liam's tense, rigid body.

'I'm going in,' he told the terrier. 'You stay on the beach.' And then, calculating just the right moment, the wolfhound waded carefully out until the water brushed his chin. He lowered his head and, with a series of savagely quick lunges and bites, snapped the bodies of fish to right and left and before him. The seal swam on past and dragged himself up on to the strand.

'Oh, Seal, what wonderful swimming!' Zoe cried in admiration. The seal honked to her in a friendly way and then waited for his partner to fetch the bounty ashore.

Liam plunged through the wavelets, carrying one load of stricken fish in his great jaws, then returned for a second. A pile began to form on the sand of writhing, gleaming bodies. When he had completed his harvest of the waves, Liam proceeded to bite some of the larger fish into pieces; the smaller ones he left alone. Then he nudged the food across the beach with his muzzle to the waiting seal.

'That's Seal's share,' he announced. 'He'll wonder what's happened. I don't usually ask him to hunt by day.'

'I'm sorry,' said Zoe. 'I'm to blame for that. I haven't eaten for so long and I—'

'Don't worry, don't worry,' Liam reassured her. '*He* won't mind eating early and neither will I. As a matter of fact Seal and I didn't eat much last night for the fish were scattered by the storm. Eat your fill now! Don't wait for me.'

Zoe did as she was bidden. The fish were icy cold, salty and delicious. She didn't pause once in her meal, but ate steadily until satisfied. The little she needed meant that the lion's share of the catch still remained for the wolfhound to eat. The seal honked comfortably and happily behind the remains of his meal. He looked at Zoe, who had so obviously enjoyed what he had provided, and honked again. There was no doubting his delight in his new companion.

Full, the two dogs went towards the cave, while the seal returned to his natural element. Zoe curled herself up inside the cave mouth and was soon asleep. Liam sat outside the cave, gazing across the water in the same fixed way he had from his pinnacle on the cliff. His mind was occupied with the problem of getting Zoe to the red ship, which might arrive at any time. From his beach, the only route to the harbour was by water. Although he hadn't warned her, Liam knew that soon Zoe would be faced with an additional problem: after feasting on saltwater fish, she would wake with a raging thirst. (Over the years his body had adjusted to this demand so that he had become more used to it.) Access to fresh water was limited, however, now that their retreat was cut off. He was thankful for the storm which must have left pools of rainwater amongst the rocks. There would be boulders with crannies and hollows where rainwater must have collected, but the only ones that would be of use would be those which had not already contained remnants of sea water to contaminate the fresh.

Liam decided he had better investigate the water available before Zoe should wake up. He would have to taste here and there until he found a reservoir of pure drinking water. Setting off at an amble across the beach, he paused now and then to sniff, his nose telling him which water was brackish. He went from rock to rock, clambering or leaping across the mounds of debris that had fallen from the cliff. He crossed the whole width of the beach, finding nothing suitable, and then returned, making an even more thorough search. There was one large boulder, smooth-sided and high, on top of which a pool of water glistened at the bottom of a deep indentation. Liam looked up at it gloomily from all sides, but couldn't see any projections by which an animal might climb up. He turned his back on the boulder, yet he knew that only rainwater could have collected to form that pool, for the tide scarcely reached the base of the rock. But it wouldn't serve their purpose. The wolfhound continued his search, sniffing here, taking just a taste of liquid there. There was nothing drinkable – no other source of fresh water. He went back to the cave to see if Zoe was awake, but she was still asleep, lying close to the pile of mementoes of his master he had gathered. Liam sat and watched her with misgiving. He didn't know what would happen when she awoke; yet even as he watched, the terrier sensed his presence, stirred, and opened her eyes.

15

Plans for Rescue

Bertram had not woken up. When the *Crest* moored close to the jetty at Multon harbour the exhausted boxer, now warm and dry, slept on. Halebury gave him a gentle pat. Bertram raised his head, blinked, recognized the seaman and got up, wiggling his hindquarters in greeting. Halebury led him up the steps by the jetty wall and they were soon back at Multon pier. The pier kiosk was, of course, closed. Halebury reminded himself of the telephone number on Bertram's collar tag. Keeping a firm grip on the piece of string he used as a lead, he took Bertram to the nearest call-box and dialled the number. There was no reply. He decided to get himself a cup of tea and a cake and ask after the Lockes at the same time.

The Seagull Café was still open and Halebury sat down at a table near the counter. Mr Clements came to take his order. He noticed Bertram sitting quietly against a table leg. 'Well!' he cried. 'Here's a surprise. Is that who I think it is?'

'It's the boxer from the kiosk if that's what you mean. And where do you think I found him?'

'I don't know, but our Zoe disappeared at the same time he did, 'Mr Clements said excitedly. 'Have you seen her?'

Halebury hedged, not wanting to raise false hopes. 'I think I may have done,' he replied. 'I'm not entirely sure. But let me tell you – *this* dog was on Clany.'

Mr Clements looked thunderstruck. 'On the island!' He looked round. 'Mabel!' he called to his wife. He turned back to the seaman. 'D'you think Zoe could be there?'

'Could be,' said Halebury. 'I've been searching for her on the island. I know your dog and this one were in the habit of running around with my Jack. When I found Bertram I wondered if he'd come over with his owner. I've just been trying to ring Mr Locke. Have you seen him around?'

'No, he and his wife have gone off on holiday. A belated one, mind you; they've been waiting around for word of Bertram here. The police couldn't help at all. We've all been searching and searching everywhere – never thought of the island.' He explained to his wife the cause of his excitement.

'It's a mystery how he – or they – got there,' Halebury remarked. 'I've been unable to find Zoe though; she may be hiding.'

'But why?' Clements said. 'Why would she want to do that?' Halebury merely shrugged.

Clements went on. 'So they both somehow got on to a boat and disappeared together. It could have been yours, Mr Halebury!'

Halebury's mouth dropped open. 'I never thought—' he began. Then he shook his head slowly. 'No, it couldn't have been on the *Crest*,' he muttered. 'Or could it?'

'We'd all given up,' Mrs Clements said and her voice caught on a sob. 'The Lockes did go away in the finish. Mr Locke was very upset, you know, but his wife seemed more angry than anything else.'

'Well, what do I do with Bertram?' Halebury asked. 'Will they be gone long?'

'Just over a week, I think, isn't it, Mabel?' Clements said. His wife nodded. 'To be truthful,' he went on, 'I don't think we've got room for him here, otherwise I'd offer to have him. The Lockes had been going to put the old creature in kennels.'

Bertram heard the word he knew and hated so much, gave a sudden, violent tug on the string and tried to pull away. Halebury was nearly dragged from his seat. He hauled Bertram back and calmed him down with a few comforting strokes. 'Look at that now,' he said in astonishment. 'Whatever set him off?'

The Clementses glanced at each other – they had guessed.

'I suppose, then,' said Halebury, following up the topic of Bertram's keep, 'you'll want *me* to look after him?'

'If you don't mind,' Mrs Clements said uncertainly. 'But, we're neglecting you.' She wiped her eyes and became brisk. 'What would you like to order?'

While Halebury was munching his cake, Mr and Mrs Clements had a talk together. Mrs Clements wanted her husband to go back to Clany with the seaman and make a search for Zoe, but he wasn't so sure that was such a good idea.

'How would I get off again?' he wanted to know. 'I couldn't bother our friend there. He's done enough already.'

'Come back on the mail packet.'

'When's that due?'

'Tomorrow.'

'But what if I haven't found Zoe? Am I to go on looking or come back on it?'

Mrs Clements pondered. 'You'd have to keep looking, don't you think, for a while? To be *sure*.'

'Yes. Well, that means staying somewhere. There aren't any hotels, are there?'

'I'm sure you could get bed and breakfast somewhere.

Seaman Halebury would help you with that.'

It seemed settled, so Mr Clements went back to their sole customer. 'When did you plan to go back to the island?' he asked him.

'As soon as I'd handed the dog over,' was the reply. 'Now he'll be making the crossing back with me, it looks like.'

'D'you mind a second passenger?' Clements asked.

'No. Who'd that be – you?'

'Yes. My wife wants me to make a thorough search for our pet. You never know, if Zoe is there, she might come to *my* call.'

'Worth a try,' Halebury nodded. 'When do you want to go then?'

'Whenever you're ready. It's your boat. You let me know and I'll be waiting.'

'All right. About an hour's time?'

'I'll go and pack a few things.'

Meanwhile, left to his own devices, Jack couldn't resist returning to the cliff path that overlooked the exposed end of the rock tunnel. He stood looking down on it, hoping, yet dreading, to see a sign of Zoe. He shuddered as he remembered that he himself had once run through that passage with Zoe and Bertram. Liam's beach wasn't visible from the cliff-top; only the accumulated debris of the landslide could be seen piled up where it had toppled and crashed. Yet Jack hung around. He had a feeling that he had been drawn to this spot for a reason and in the end, he did see something.

From high up he caught sight of the seal swimming in the clear water, just below the surface. And then, as he watched the animal thread its way through the dark swathes of weed, he saw Liam breasting the little waves, coming to a stop just as he was about to be caught by the tide. He saw the driving and killing of the fish and then watched Liam leave the sea, his jaws full of food. The significance of this daytime hunt did not pass Jack by. He was sure some of that food was for Zoe, though he never actually saw her. He ran back once more to his master's cottage: it was deserted. Then Jack had an idea – there were other humans who might help him. He headed for the farm where his little friend lived.

Luckily the girl and her mother were both in the garden. Jack pushed himself under the gate and, ignoring the child's invitation to play, started barking urgently. When the little girl heard the noise, she put her thumb in her mouth and backed away, not understanding Jack's summons and a little frightened by it. As soon as the dog had her mother's attention, he ran to the gate and barked again, looking back to see if she would follow. The woman was puzzled at first, but Jack was so insistent she eventually realized he wanted to show her something. She called to her husband who was examining the damage caused to his produce by the storm.

'Bob! Can you come a minute? It's Halebury's dog. I think something's happened.'

The farmer came, squelching through the mud in his boots. Jack greeted him by going through the same routine as before. 'I'd better go,' the man said. 'Perhaps his master's hurt.' He opened the garden gate.

Jack dashed out, still barking, and ran off along the footpath. He returned to make sure the man was following and then raced ahead, diving through the brown, sodden fronds of overhanging bracken. The farmer soon realized he was being taken in the direction away from Halebury's cottage. He wondered what had happened to the seaman. Was he in difficulties at sea? No, surely his dog would have been with him. But something serious must have happened.

So, while Halebury was actually en route for Multon with Bertram on board, his dog Jack was leading another man towards Zoe in the hope of getting her rescued. The farmer, whose name was Patterson, was tall and lean and took long strides, keeping up pretty well with the eager mongrel. At last they came across the top of the island along the cliff path. Patterson began to look about him closely and to tread warily, which made Jack impatient. He barked at the delay, and as they neared the cliff edge where the landslide had occurred, he became more and more excited. Patterson felt sure there must have been an accident. He saw where the cliff had been torn away and fully expected to see the body of Halebury over the edge. Testing the ground thoroughly, he inched forward, Jack barking encouragement. Patterson peered over, keeping his distance from the steep drop. He shook his head at the piles of fallen rock and debris, but saw no body. What he did see was a great wolfhound, climbing through the rocks and boulders as if searching for something. Jack barked again, calling to Zoe, but his voice was lost on the breeze and was unheard on the beach. Liam didn't look up and Zoe remained hidden in the cave.

Patterson wasn't familiar with the giant dog who had kept watch for so long from his pinnacle. He imagined that Jack was alerting him to this dog's existence – a dog who appeared to have lost, and was now searching for, his master. It wasn't the accident the farmer had been expecting, but maybe there was a body down there, or an injured man buried amongst the rubble. He walked cautiously up and down, trying to see a route down the cliffside that might offer a possibility, however difficult, of climbing down to the beach. There was nothing at all. The only way of getting to that place was from the sea.

Patterson knew he must investigate and Halebury's mongrel dog, who had so cleverly led him to the spot, gave him a clue. He must contact the seaman and ask him to ferry him to that lonely beach, without delay. To Jack's dismay the farmer turned on his heel and, with the utmost haste, strode away. The dog barked and barked in vain. He was desperately frustrated by the man's disappearance, after he had got him to come this far, and his barks turned to ones of fury.

'All right, boy, come on. I'll see to it. Come on now,' the farmer called and whistled to Jack to follow. The mongrel trotted after him dispiritedly and fell farther and farther behind. He wanted to remain near the scene of devastation, to see Zoe, reassure her that he knew of her plight, and tell her somehow he would save her. But he didn't know what the farmer intended to do and, in case he still meant to help in some way, he decided to keep the man in sight.

Zoe had woken and, just as Liam had expected, immediately asked, 'Where can I drink?'

Liam said, 'I've just been looking for water myself. There doesn't seem to be any close by.'

Zoe was aghast. 'No water! After that storm?!'

'The rain ran into the sand, you see, and on the rocks it's undrinkable. Salt – like the sea.'

'But what are we to do then?'

'I wish I knew,' the wolfhound answered, genuinely worried.

'Oh,' Zoe wailed, 'why did I ever come to this horrible island?'

'Don't fret,' Liam said with false confidence, 'we'll find water.'

'Is there none in the cave? Where do you usually drink?'

'That's the problem, you see. Up on the cliffs there were usually puddles, but we can't get to those now.' He wandered around the cave, looking for any stones or rocks that might have gathered some moisture. He was merely going through the motions, though – he knew perfectly well the cave was bone dry. It was entirely weatherproof and he had chosen it for that very purpose.

Zoe watched him, her mouth as dry as the cave itself. She got up, unable to lie still any longer, ambled to the back of the cavern and looked into the rocky tunnel. She stepped into it, while Liam busied himself scouring the cave's interior. Zoe went slowly along the passage, her muzzle almost flat against the rock floor as she looked for signs of dampness. The tunnel yielded nothing but she pressed on, and soon could see light at the end of the passage. She reached the opening and looked down from a dizzying height to the rock-strewn beach. Withdrawing hastily, she suddenly noticed, in cleft at the side of the tunnel, a little liquid. The rock glistened with dampness, and she put out her tongue to taste the water. It was cold and delicious. She lapped greedily but the quantity was so small that it only irritated her thirst without quenching it and there were no other pockets of rainwater. She heard Liam's booming bark calling her and disconsolately, returned to the cave.

'Thank goodness you're safe,' he greeted her with obvious relief. 'That passage is very dangerous now, Zoe.'

'Yes,' she said. 'I'm surrounded by danger; I don't know which way to turn. What should I do?'

'You must get to the red ship when it comes,' Liam replied. 'Can you swim?'

'Yes I can, a little.'

'Could you swim to the harbour?'

'I don't know where it is. Is it far?'

'Very far for a little terrier.'

'Then I couldn't, could I?'

'Perhaps with help?' Liam looked at her, pointedly.

Zoe thought he meant to assist her. 'You're very kind,' she began, 'but I don't see how—'

'You mistake me,' the wolfhound corrected her. 'Remember Bertram? It's Seal who would help you.'

'Yes,' said Zoe slowly. 'Perhaps he could – carry me?'

'Seal would see you didn't sink,' Liam assured her. 'He's a powerful swimmer and could buoy you up, keep you afloat. But would you tire?'

'Of course I would,' she answered. 'And I may die of thirst anyway before that ship arrives.'

'If it was your only chance, would you try to swim?' Liam prompted.

'I'd have no choice. But Liam, I'm not the only trapped animal,' Zoe said unselfishly. 'How will you survive without water?'

'I'll manage somehow,' he mumbled. 'And if not – why should I care, without my master?'

'Because Seal depends on you,' Zoe reminded him.

'Yes,' Liam sighed. 'Seal depends on me.'

'And anyway,' Zoe said '*I* care what happens to you.'

16

Thirst

At three o'clock, Clements climbed aboard the *Crest*, carrying a small case. While Seaman Halebury steered a direct course for Clany harbour, Clements sat below, talking to Bertram, who was stowed safely in the cabin.

The boxer no longer understood what was happening to him. He was being shunted to and fro without apparent reason. In Multon he had expected to see his owners, but no, and now he was back on the water once more. He was in the care of humans again and passively allowed his fate to rest in their hands. How could he, an old, tired animal, influence events when humans were by? It was absurd to think so. He had made his one bid for independence and look what had happened! If it hadn't been for a kindly sea creature he would have drowned. Much as he longed for Zoe to be reunited with him, he realized this could only come about if the humans willed it. He listened to Clements' chatter and feebly wagged his hindquarters. The man was gentle and friendly, as was Jack's master, and Bertram knew he had nothing to fear.

As the *Crest* neared Clany Harbour, Patterson, the farmer, was knocking on Halebury's cottage door. Jack hung back, awaiting developments. Patterson knocked three times, then he stomped around the building, looking in through the windows. Of course the cottage was empty. He wondered what to do: who else might have a boat handy? He must go to the harbour and find out. Patterson marched back home, told his wife the gist of his errand and set off again, Jack still following at a distance. He was forgotten now.

Clements and Halebury, leading Bertram, disembarked. The seaman had already said that Zoe's owner could stay at his cottage until he had completed his search for the missing terrier, so the two men walked slowly away from the harbour to the house. Bertram plodded along, his flabby stomach swinging from side to side. He was still very tired and Halebury, well aware of this, didn't force the pace. Ten minutes later they came face to face with Patterson, Jack hovering in the distance.

'Just the man!' the farmer cried. 'Mr Halebury, I need your help. More to the point, someone else does. Someone in trouble.'

Halebury and Clements glanced at each other. 'What is it?' the seaman asked. 'I was just on my way home.'

'There's been a cliff fall,' Patterson explained. 'In the storm. I think there's been a bad accident. I've seen a dog – a huge thing, bigger than a Great Dane – wandering along an isolated part of the beach just below the landslide. I'm sure his owner's been hurt or. . . .' He left the rest unsaid.

'What can I do to help?' Halebury asked.

'We need a boat,' Patterson explained. 'I'm sorry,' he continued, turning to the stranger, Clements, 'but it *is* urgent.'

'Of course, I understand.'

Halebury said to Clements, 'Do you want to have a scout around for a while? I won't be too long. If there's anything to find on that beach – well, we won't be long finding it.'

'Certainly, go ahead,' said Mr Clements. 'I can start looking for Zoe right here. I have to begin somewhere.'

'See you later,' said Seaman Halebury. 'Er, could you look after Bertram for a spell?'

'I'd be glad to,' was the reply. 'He might give me a clue.'

Halebury and Patterson were soon in the *Crest*. Across the water they heard Clements calling his pet's name. 'Zo-e! Zo-e!'

Halebury brought his boat close to Liam's cove. He could soon see the devastation wrought by the storm, gave a low whistle and muttered to himself. He cut the engine of the *Crest* and, as she drifted in, scanned the shoreline through his binoculars. Liam and Zoe were inside the cave, but the men on the boat were concentrating on searching the beach.

Patterson waited. Then he said, 'Anything there?'

'I can't see any bodies,' Halebury answered bluntly, handing him the glasses.

'No,' the other eventually agreed. 'Not at first sight. And – funny thing – I can't see the dog now either.'

'Like a Great Dane, you said?'

'Yes, only hairier and bigger.'

Halebury suggested, 'He may be behind a rock.'

Patterson took the glasses from his eyes and the two men exchanged solemn looks. Halebury put their thoughts into words. 'Yes,' he said, 'there may be something else hidden too.'

He let the *Crest* ride in closer, then anchored, and lowered the dinghy. 'We'll have to go in,' he said unnecessarily. Soon the two men were rowing to the shore. They jumped out and began their search, looking systematically behind and between each boulder. They went in one direction as far as they could, up to the sheer rock face. Then they turned and went towards the cave, stepping carefully so as not to miss anything.

'If there was a body,' said Patterson, 'I suppose it could have been washed out to sea.'

'It could have been,' agreed Halebury. 'Or, if there's an injured man, he might have crawled in there.' He jerked a thumb at the cave entrance.

They said no more until they had combed the strand right up to the cavern. It was very dark when they went inside. The two dogs were at the back of the cave and the men, temporarily blinded by the deep gloom, could see nothing. Eventually they did see, just inside, the pile of relics Liam had collected and lovingly guarded for so long. Patterson went towards it. 'Here – look at this!' he cried.

Halebury just had time to notice the little heap before the two men were startled out of their wits. From the black depths of the cave, the wolfhound leapt to defend these only mementoes of his master, fearing the men intended to remove them. Halebury and Patterson were assailed by a furious giant of a dog who appeared, as it were, from nowhere, baring its teeth and barking deafeningly. They backed away and, in the face of this unexpected assault, hurried back to the dinghy, considerably shaken. Liam ran after them, driving them into the sea. The men piled into the dinghy and, neither of them able to say a word, rowed back to the *Crest*. Liam watched them. He stood in the water, the hackles lifted along his back, and stayed there until he was sure he had seen them off. Only then did the two men recover their voices.

'It's – it's mad or something,' Patterson stammered.

'Dangerous, too,' Halebury commented. His face was

white. 'I really thought it was going to savage us.'

'It was ready to.'

Both men breathed hard.

'What if the body's inside the cave then?' Halebury said eventually. 'We wouldn't be able to touch it, would we?'

'No,' Patterson agreed. 'It'll need more men than two to tackle that beast and hold it down.'

They stared at the wolfhound who still lingered on the shore, glaring balefully, in case they should try another move. Zoe, meanwhile, had kept well out of sight, feeling frightened herself. And only a short distance away on the other side of the island, Mr Clements, her owner, was searching in vain for her.

Bertram was exhausted by his experiences that day and Clements could tell he was in no fit state to be walked about for long. He was glad when he saw the *Crest* returning to the harbour and Halebury and Patterson disembark.

'This animal needs a place to rest,' Clements said at once. He felt a duty towards his neighbour's dog.

'Yes,' said Seaman Halebury. 'I wouldn't mind a rest myself.' He described his experience in the cove to Clements, with Mr Patterson adding to the story. The café owner's eyes popped: he was quite definitely alarmed.

'I hope my Zoe hasn't come across such a wild beast, if she *is* on the island,' he said nervously. 'How could it be allowed to roam free like that?'

Halebury shook his head. 'There used to be a wolfhound that sailed with a fisherman friend I had, a man who was lost at sea some years ago. But his dog was as docile and quiet as this one is savage.'

He turned to Patterson and they discussed arrangements to meet the next day and round up a few other helpers, for they were both sure that the dangerous dog should be quickly dealt with. Then they went their own way.

Halebury led Clements to his cottage. It took them quite a while, for Bertram was so tired they had to walk at a snail's pace. By the time they got there they both felt in need of refreshment, and sipped mugs of strong tea while Bertram, who had gratefully lapped up some warm milk, snored on the carpet. They hadn't been settled long when Jack announced his arrival by a couple of sharp yaps. Halebury went to open the door. The mongrel had kept the men in sight all along and had even heard Liam's furious barking when his cave had been entered. Then he had followed his master and the stranger home, half expecting to see Zoe already in the cottage.

Jack greeted his master, sniffed at the sleeping Bertram and, realizing that his attempts to get help for Zoe had failed, turned his attention to food. He knew he had left some meat uneaten in the kitchen that morning and went to devour it. It had gone. Guessing that the boxer was responsible, he growled resentfully. Halebury knew he wanted feeding, finished his tea and quickly scraped together a meal for the dog. Jack was very hungry, for he'd been running to and fro since early morning, and wolfed the contents of his bowl in a series of gulps.

'Greedy!' Halebury cautioned him.

Clements was stirring in the other room. 'Not much daylight left,' he remarked as Halebury came back. 'I'll go and start my search again, unhampered.' He meant, without Bertram.

'Oh, will you? I'll show you the path then,' said the seaman. 'It'd be best for you to try around the village first.' He set Clements on his way, giving him all the necessary directions.

'You'll know your way back?' he asked.

'I will,' said the café owner. 'And let's hope I won't be on my own.'

When Liam had eventually returned to the cave, Zoe had calmed down but was suffering agonies of thirst.

'Why did you drive them off?' she reproached the great dog. 'They might have helped me.'

All other considerations had been driven out of Liam's mind when he thought his master's things were about to be disturbed, but now he saw he hadn't helped Zoe, and had perhaps even prevented her from being rescued.

'I didn't think,' he admitted hollowly. 'I see now I've done you harm. But, Zoe, if it's any comfort, I think the men will come back.'

'What good will that be to me?' she demanded. 'You'd only terrorize them again.'

'Not if they keep away from my master's things,' Liam replied. 'And I'm going to move them out of their reach.' As Zoe watched him with a mixture of bewilderment and compassion, he carried each piece – the pipe, the shreds of clothing, the boot – to the back of the cave and up into the rocky passage that now led nowhere.

'They'll never think of looking there,' said the wolfhound afterwards with satisfaction. So important were these sad items to him, he thought they held a magical significance for any other creature, too, human as well as animal. 'And so,' he continued, 'you'll be free to go with them.'

'I can't just remain here and wait,' Zoe protested. 'I have to get to somewhere with water.'

'Yes, we both need that,' he agreed. 'I've looked outside, smelling every pool and puddle. All salt. But we'll look again to make sure; I may have missed something, after all. Will you come with me?'

'Of course. What else can I do?'

Liam crept along the beach, pausing to sniff at everything, though he held out no hope of finding water. He didn't think he had missed any possibility before, but he knew he simply must try once more for Zoe's sake. She trotted after him trustingly, relying entirely on his judgment. The wolfhound was so painstaking in examining every tiny pool of water that Zoe began to feel confident; but when, time and time again, he rejected each one and moved on, she found this confidence waning. At last there was only the one boulder left to search, the high smooth rock, on top of which a clear, glistening liquid lay tantalizingly out of reach. Liam turned to the little white terrier with a grave look.

'I'm afraid there *is* no water, except in the place we can't reach,' he summed up.

'Why can't we reach it?' she demanded.

Liam indicated the great rock. 'Could you jump that high?'

'Don't be silly,' she answered, angrily. Her tremendous thirst caused her to vent her temper. 'I'm the midget of the two. You're the giant. Can't you do something?'

'What do you suggest, Zoe? I can't reach the top. And, even if I could, how would that help you?'

'Oh, I just can't stand this,' Zoe wailed. 'I've got to do something or I'll run mad.' She had indeed begun to look wild-eyed.

Liam was alarmed. 'I'll call Seal,' he said. 'It's all I can think of. I hope he hasn't gone too far out. You'll have to try and swim for the harbour, there's simply no other way. Seal will bear you along.' Without waiting for a reply he bounded into the surf and, raising his head, howled long and high. He repeated this special sound at intervals and, after each repetition, he scanned the expanse of blue water for a sign of his friend's bobbing head.

Zoe lay down in despair. She didn't think the seal would come until nightfall and listened to Liam's mournful calls of distress with an uneasy shiver. She thought of Bertram and Jack, both of whom had as good as deserted her, and felt the most overwhelming loneliness and regret. Such a short time ago she had been the lively West Highland White on the beach at Multon, playing games with her two friends and, as she now accepted, without a care in the world. How could she have known what would come from their misguided adventure? Jack was to blame chiefly, she knew that. But she blamed herself too, for being fascinated by his high spirits, even though she had only slow, well-meaning, dear old Bertram to compare him with.

'Seal's coming!' Liam suddenly boomed. 'I can see his head popping up to find me.'

Zoe raced to his side. The ripples nearly covered her short-legged body. She could make out nothing at first but, as the seal came swiftly onwards, she saw him and entered the water, dog-paddling vigorously, eager to begin her journey at once.

'You're going in the wrong direction,' Liam barked at her. He waded out farther and nosed her on to the correct course. The seal came round behind her, glancing at the wolfhound for an explanation. Liam decided the simplest way to tell the seal what they wanted was to swim along with Zoe himself, making it obvious that he was helping her. He knew Seal would soon understand. And so they went, Zoe's little legs paddling nineteen to the dozen. Liam made great headway through the last of the tide and then, with a nudge of his head or shoulder, he helped to propel the terrier along and into the open sea. It was calm and the water not too cold, for the summer's warmth hadn't yet left it. Seal swam around the two in a joyful manner, sometimes getting underneath Zoe's tiny body and raising her slightly, easing her gallant efforts by making his slippery back a temporary raft.

Liam soon saw he was no longer needed, and bellowed to Zoe, 'Keep on the same course – don't veer. Seal will see you to the harbour. Good luck!' Then he turned and swam powerfully back to the shore. He was determined to be around to stop any further attempts to rob him of his master's belongings.

Strangely enough, despite the wolfhound's disappearance, Zoe wasn't frightened. She had the utmost confidence in Seal, whom she knew had already saved Bertram from drowning. Little by little, in the waning light, her white speck of soaked fur ate up the daunting distance separating her from Clany harbour. An end to her misery was also in view.

17

Dog in the Cave

Clements, the café owner, met with no luck in Clany village. No one to whom he spoke could give him any clues and, call Zoe as he might, he was never answered. As he looked hopelessly around, his lost pet was being carried through the water at express pace for the last few hundred metres towards the jetty steps. The terrier's valiant journey had finally exhausted her and the seal, understanding this only too well, had buoyed her along. With a few lazy flicks of his tail, swimming just beneath her, he completed her journey for her. Seal then sensibly pushed her up on to the exposed steps above the water line. No humans were about in the early evening gloom and, with his customary honks of farewell, the seal swam away. He had done all he could.

Presently Zoe recovered. She staggered up the steps and there, on top of the jetty, was a large puddle of water. She cautiously sniffed at it. It was fresh. Immediately she took the longest drink she had ever swallowed at one time. As soon as she had refreshed her burning throat, she recalled that the wolfhound was suffering in the same way as she had been. How would he find comfort? She knew it was her turn now to find help. Liam had made her freedom possible – now he had to be rescued before he went mad with thirst. Zoe felt a new animal now and, with her great purpose firmly in mind, she set off for the monastery and the Good People.

It wasn't far away – nowhere was on this small island. As she neared the monastery, Zoe suddenly felt as if she had been transported back in time to her own home and its familiar surroundings. She heard the sound of her master's call. Zoe stopped dead; she couldn't account for it. But the sound was repeated, again and again, and it seemed to be coming closer. She gave an answering yap and, gathering her little legs together, bounded in the direction of this unexpected noise. As she approached the home of the Good People, Mr Clements abruptly emerged from behind a screen of trees. He saw a white blur in the dusk, moving swiftly towards him. It was like a dream. His voice broke on his pet's name.

'Zo – e?' he almost whispered. But there was no mistaking her now. Still drenched from her long swim, thinner, and with her white fur now matted and, indeed, not so white as he had always known it, Zoe came. Despite her changed appearance, Clements knew at once he had found his long-lost pet. In a moment they were reunited; she leapt up, he caught her in his arms and hugged her.

'I knew you must be here, I knew it,' he murmured to the little dog, over and over again.

In just a short while they were at Halebury's cottage. The seaman was almost as delighted for Clements' sake as Zoe's owner was himself. Bertram and Jack greeted the terrier joyfully in their individual ways but, in Zoe's mind, there was no doubting which of the two was her more genuine friend. She was given a good rub down, a clean up, some food, and then she drank an entire bowl of fresh water. The beach dogs were together again, as night was falling outside the cottage.

'You'll be going back on the mail boat,' Halebury said to his visitor.

'Yes. What time does it sail?'

'It docks at the island mid-morning. Usually stays an hour or two.'

'I'll be waiting. And you have another job to do?'

'Yes,' said Halebury. 'The wolfhound. I seem to have lumbered myself there. I'll be leaving with you to meet the farmer, and we'll need a few men to deal with the brute.'

'*Is* the dog so dangerous?' Clements asked.

'Frightened, very likely. But he can't be left.'

'What will you do with him?'

'I don't know. There's a vet on the island. He'll have to sedate him. But after that. . . .' He shook his head.

The three dogs, left to their own devices in the kitchen, swapped stories. None of them had any idea what fate awaited Liam.

The next day, the Halebury household was up and about early. Mr Clements was eager to get back to the café and to his wife, bringing the wonderful news with him. Seaman Halebury cooked breakfast, and later that morning Clements and Zoe and Halebury and Jack left the cottage. They made their farewells. Poor Bertram was alone once more; he couldn't understand why he and Zoe were being separated again. Inside the cottage he whined and barked in the greatest distress, but his ordeal wasn't over yet.

The café owner and his newly-washed pet got off safely on the mail packet and were soon home again in the Seagull Café. Mrs Clements was overjoyed to see them and Zoe realized that the home she had known for so long was not the cramped, loveless place she had believed it to be, but the most comfortable, secure and peaceful haven any dog could wish for. She thought continually about Liam and how luck had treated him, only wishing he could be as fortunate as herself.

Back on Clany, four men were disembarking from the *Crest* for Liam's cove – Halebury, Patterson, the vet and another man, a fisherman. There was no sign anywhere of the wolfhound as the men trudged warily along the beach.

'He's in the cave all right,' Patterson remarked when the fisherman expressed some doubt. 'We must all go together and seize him.'

Seaman Halebury held a powerful torch. They all wore stout gloves and the vet was carrying his instruments and drugs in a coat pocket. The fisherman had a piece of net-ting with him. They entered the cave cautiously, and Halebury shone the torch along the walls and into the back of the cave. They could immediately tell there was no human body anywhere.

Liam had heard their approach and was inside the tunnel, guarding his master's things. On board the *Crest*, Jack waited for Halebury's return.

The fisherman looked at the farmer quizzically. 'In the cave?' he repeated ironically.

Patterson was puzzled. 'Where else could he be?' He turned to Halebury as if for guidance, but he just shrugged.

'Give me the torch,' said the farmer. He grasped it and advanced deep into the cave, sweeping the beam across every nook and cranny. Suddenly the gaping hole of the passage entrance was revealed and held by the torchlight. Patterson caught his breath, then let it out slowly. 'So that's it,' he muttered, turning and beckoning the others forward. Together they crept to the tunnel and, from inside the passage, Liam growled low in his throat: it was a warning.

The men were flummoxed. The opening of the tunnel was too narrow for them to seize the animal.

'Could we coax him out?' the fisherman asked.

'With what?' retorted Patterson. 'Mr Branch' – he spoke to the vet – 'you know most about animals. Can you do anything?'

'No more than any of you,' he answered, 'if I can't get close enough to inject him.'

'Perhaps we should leave him be,' the fisherman said dubiously.

'No. Leave it to me,' Patterson answered. He shone the torch up into the rock tunnel where Liam was lying, on top of the relics he had carried there. He bared his teeth at the farmer but made no other move. Patterson recoiled, but not before he had noticed the tobacco pipe. He was reminded of the previous day, and turned to Halebury.

'D'you remember that collection of things we discovered at the cave entrance? Just before we were attacked?'

Halebury nodded.

'I believe the dog's moved them into this tunnel. He – he's guarding them!'

Seaman Halebury took a look from a safe distance. 'I believe you're right, Mr Patterson.'

'Well, this must mean something! A pipe! Must belong to his master.'

'*That's* why he attacked us,' said Halebury. 'He tried to drive us away. But if it's the dog I'm beginning to think it is, this pile of oddments is all that's left of his master.'

His words put a different complexion on the situation. From being a savage, dangerous beast the wolfhound had now become something the men could pity.

'Poor creature,' said Mr Branch, the vet. 'How long has he been surviving here on his own?'

Halebury shook his head. 'I wouldn't like to say, but certainly too long for his own good.'

The vet nodded. He felt this poor stray was more his

responsibility than that of the others. He squatted down and began talking softly and kindly to the wary animal. Liam listened and swallowed uncertainly: it was an age since he had heard the persuasive power of a compassionate human voice. But he remained where he was, keeping jealous hold of his treasures. The vet could see these tactics wouldn't draw the dog out of his lair.

'This won't work,' he announced, 'but he can't stay in there for ever. I suggest we withdraw to the beach and then – just wait.'

The others weren't so sure. 'It could be a long wait,' said Patterson. 'I can't hang around all day.'

'Nor can I,' the fisherman added.

'None of us can,' said the vet. 'But let's try it for a while?'

The others agreed, and they sat about on boulders away from the cave entrance. They hadn't much to say. Jack yapped frustratedly from the boat but Halebury called to him to be quiet. The mongrel couldn't understand what they were waiting for and kept running up and down the *Crest*'s length. Liam heard Jack's yaps carried faintly to him in the depths of the cave. He was puzzled by the men's behaviour. If they wanted his master's relics, why had they retreated? He lay in acute discomfort and pondered. Unlike Zoe, his violent thirst hadn't been quenched and during the night he and the seal had shared their customary meal. The salt fish had only made his agony worse. He knew the men could take him to water, and the kindly one had sounded as if he had wanted to help. Should he allow him to? He certainly needed help from someone. After a while in the continuing silence, Liam's curiosity got the better of him. He crept out of the tunnel and, little by little, pausing frequently to listen with his head on one side, he advanced to the cave entrance. As soon as his head showed beyond the mouth of the cave, the men pounced. He was pinned down by six strong arms under the net and the vet quickly slid his needle into the dog's rump. In a short while the wolfhound's struggles were stilled.

Patterson and Branch carried him to the dinghy, the others following. On board the *Crest*, Jack, more excited than ever, waited impatiently for them. Unconscious and wrapped in the net, Liam wasn't recognized by the mongrel.

'What now?' asked the fisherman.

'I'll see to him,' said the vet. 'He'll have to be penned securely. He'll come round in a couple of hours and he might prove difficult.'

None of the men wanted to interfere; they regarded their part in the incident as over. What the vet would do with the great dog in the future was his business. The *Crest* returned to the harbour and they went their separate ways, once they had helped Mr Branch with his burden as far as the surgery.

In Halebury's cottage Jack and Bertram came to an understanding. Bertram was glad to be left alone no longer and, without Zoe, the rivalry that had existed between them was over. Neither dog understood why they were suddenly living together, but as far as they could tell, this was to be the new arrangement and they accepted it. They were fed together and exercised together. Bertram forgot all about the Good People and only occasionally wondered if he would ever see his real owners again. At any rate life with Seaman Halebury and his mongrel was better than living in the detested kennels.

18

A Conclusion

Later on the day that Liam was rescued, he awoke and found his strength returning. He discovered he was in a large pen, with plenty of room to move about, but surrounded by a high wooden fence. All was quiet. He stood up, staggered a little, but managed to keep his feet, and looked around. The first things he noticed were dishes of food and water. He moved shakily but as quickly as he could to the water bowl, and drained it. He felt better and, gradually, remembered what had happened to him and why he was shut in. He ate the food and then lay down again until he was confident his full vigour was restored. He didn't know where he was, but he knew that somehow he must escape. The relics of his master were left unguarded. Shut in this cage, he couldn't keep his watch for his master's return. There was also Seal to think about – he wouldn't understand his disappearance.

Liam jumped up and paced all round the pen, sniffing at it and examining it for weaknesses. Then he looked up, trying to assess the fence's height. He trotted away a short distance on his long legs and turned, then ran at the fence and sprang up. It was too high to scale and he dropped back on all fours. However, the fence had shaken considerably under the wolfhound's weight and power. Liam was encouraged by this and now adopted a new tactic.

He charged the fence and hurled himself with all his strength directly against it. The palings cracked; they were high but not stout. In another moment he had broken through. One side of his body was scored by broken woodwork which left sharp splinters in his thick grey coat, but Liam didn't care. He was in the open. For a moment he stopped, unsure of his bearings. Just then, alarmed by the sharp 'crack!' of the fence, two of the vet's assistants rushed out from the surgery. Liam saw them and took to his heels. He soon realized the route he must take to his cave, and his long powerful legs, with their loping strides, quickly left his human pursuers stranded and panting for breath. He raced for the cliff-top, and before long, reached the point where he overlooked his cove.

Now the great dog was faced with the worst sort of dilemma. The only route down was a chance leap out into space, in the hope that some of the debris from the fallen cliff would break his fall. He cared nothing for the risk, but if he should injure himself badly, he wouldn't be able to reach his cave and its precious contents. He paused only for a moment and then sprang downwards. He landed awkwardly, one leg striking a large rock. He yelped shrilly with the shock and pain, but the other three legs had found a softer base of piled soil and turf. He struggled forward, dragging himself tumbling and scrabbling down on to the beach. His painful hind leg bumped along the ground as he lurched forward on three legs. Now, dizzy with the constant pain and wet with blood from a gash on his chest, Liam staggered to the cave. Somehow he managed to creep to the rear of the cave, and, at the entrance to the rocky passage, he saw with relief that his master's relics were untouched. He fell across the entrance, with his body half in the passage and half out of it, exhausted. Now all that remained was to wait for his master. He would never leave the relics again.

A little over a week later, the *Crest* sailed again from Clany. This time Bertram was on his way to rejoin his owners in Multon. Jack was on board too, and the two dogs stood in the stern, looking across to Liam's cove as they passed by the beach. 'I wonder where Liam watches for his master now?' murmured Bertram.

'Who knows?' said Jack. 'Perhaps his vigil is over.'

'I'd like to think that his master will come back for him some day,' said Bertram, softly.

But Jack turned from the scene, already losing interest as the boat chugged further out to sea.